Good-bye, Chicago

1928: End of an Era

W. R. Burnett

❧

ST. MARTIN'S PRESS
New York

For information, write: St. Martin's Press,
175 Fifth Avenue, New York, N.Y. 10010
Manufactured in the United States of America
Library of Congress Cataloging in Publication Data
Burnett, William Riley, 1899–
Goodbye Chicago.
I. Title
PS3503.U6258G6 813'.52 80–27564
ISBN 0–312–33851–1
Design by Dennis J. Grastorf

10 9 8 7 6 5 4 3 2 1

FIRST EDITION

For Whitney, again

NIGHT. City Fire Boat X3 was moving in toward the dock from the middle of the river when the wheelman spotted what looked like a floating bundle of old clothes. Orders were given; a boat was lowered, and two firemen worked briefly with a boat hook and net, finally managing to get the body aboard. Beyond them were the lights of The Loop, reflected here and there in fractured patches all over the black water, while just beyond and high above them towered the office buildings, dark except for their lighted elevator shafts. To their left traffic hummed across the Wacker Street Bridge, headlights flashing.

It was just another night. But not for the dead woman, who was now reduced to resembling a bundle of old clothes.

&

DETECTIVE DAVE SANTORELLI came leisurely down the hallway, smoking a cigarette and trying to shake the sleep out of his eyes. They'd had a bad night with the kid, high fever, and telephone instructions from the doctor, who had seemed sore as hell at being disturbed at two A.M. Well . . . the doc had been right at that. An hour later the fever had left the kid, her temperature had dropped to normal, and while they fumed, she slept, smiling slightly. To make matters worse the two older kids had been up and down all night long, unable to sleep, wanting to help, not knowing what to do.

Dave often wondered if he'd done right to remarry after his first wife passed on. Now here he was with two kids, fourteen and twelve, and another one barely a year old, and a young wife who not only had a baby on her hands but two teens who were not exactly models of deportment or easy to handle. Not that they were bad kids—they were just kids, trying to find themselves as individuals, not just members of a family, and not even realizing it. A tough situation. But what about the alternatives? Celibacy? Dave was hardly in the monk class, though he had an aunt who was a nun. Whores? Nothing but trouble there, especially for a police officer. Just sleeping around promiscuously? But kids had sharp eyes, and as he well knew, falsely "ideal" pictures of their dad. To the teens, Dave knew, he was hardly a man like other men at all. They expected a lot of him. Well . . . what are you going to do . . . ?

As soon as Dave opened the squad-room door, a brother detective gestured abruptly with head and shoulders. Dave needed no other prompting but crossed to the lieutenant's door, tapped briefly, and entered. The lieutenant's name was Maheny and he had the face of a prizefighter (behind his back he was known as Sluggo). And Sluggo ran the Downtown Precinct, no doubt about it, and was considered to be one of the best administrative officers in the CPD. Captain Pfister, a friend of the mayor and a lofty figure, was seldom seen or heard. He sat behind closed doors in his big second-floor office, or he attended luncheons and spoke at political rallies. He set "policy," and that was about the extent of his duties. Sluggo ran the show.

"Sit down, Dave. I've got a tough one," said

Maheny, messing around with the papers on his desk for a moment, then leaning back and lighting a cigar. "Did you know Joe Ricordi?"

"Yes," said Dave after a moment's thought. "We were raised in the same neighborhood and we were at the Police Academy together. But we were never friends. Just said hello. His family went to my church, St. Dominick's."

"Did you ever hear anything about his wife?"

"No."

"Well . . ." said Maheny. "This one is delicate. And since you and Joe are fellow Italians . . ."

Maheny smoked in silence, staring at his desk, and Dave waited. He was used to Maheny and his slow processes of thought. So he sat trying to remember anything he could about Joe Ricordi: at the Police Academy he'd been known as the Happy Paisano—a medium-size, strong, wiry young Italian-American with curly black hair, broad high cheekbones, black eyes that danced when he laughed and flashed when he occasionally lost his temper . . . a very nice guy who was well liked, even by the Irish, who were inclined not to care too much for the "dagos" any more than some of the Italians cared for their brother Catholics, the "micks."

Dave was of mixed blood, with an Italian father and a Scotch-Irish mother. His first name was all wrong for an Italian, and he was much larger and far lighter in pigmentation than most of his compatriots. Although his last name always put Dave in the Italian-American class, he didn't seem Italian-American to himself—just American. However, he had no intention of arguing with Sluggo about the "fellow Italian" bit.

"We need a real identification," said Maheny finally. "So I'd like to have you take Sergeant Ricordi over to the city morgue."

Maheny broke off. Long pause.

"That's it?" asked Dave finally, feeling a little nervous and irritable because of his all-but-sleepless night.

"No," said Maheny. "That's not it. This may be murder—and it's your baby. She was dead before somebody put her in the water. Cause: an overdose of narcotics. She was dead, you understand . . . so she couldn't very well have put herself in the water."

Maheny was inclined to belabor the obvious, but he almost always managed to get the job done.

"You mean you've got a partial?"

"You can call it that," said Maheny. "A guy at the morgue thought he recognized her. He lived in Joe's neighborhood. She was married to Joe for seven years, and then she left him, so this guy said. Left him with two small kids. Nobody ever seemed to know what happened to her. That was about three years ago."

Long pause.

"So," said Maheny, "if we get a positive and the final coroner's report points to murder—it's yours."

"Thanks," said Dave.

"Oh, I know it might turn out to be a bad one . . . but since you and Ricordi are fellow. . . ."

He let it hang. Dave rose, gestured, and left.

⊷§

AT FIRST, largely out of weariness, Dave had decided that he'd phone Sergeant Joe Ricordi and meet him at the downtown city morgue. But he thought better of it. If this really was Joe's ex-wife, it was going to be a hell of a shock, and handling it over the phone would seem like an indignity, especially from a fellow officer, not to mention a "fellow Italian." So he drove out to the Northwest Precinct where Joe was an administrative, a desk officer, actually third in command—oh, the Happy Paisano had done well—and found him sitting in his shirtsleeves poring over a stack of paperwork, the bane of the policeman's existence.

Dave got a shock. He hardly knew Joe. This was not the Joe he remembered. The new Joe was a tough-looking, hard-eyed guy with gray at the side of his hair, though he couldn't have been over forty—same as Dave. He looked up blankly at Dave, no recognition showing in his eyes.

"I'm Dave Santorelli," said Dave. "Downtown—remember?"

Joe still didn't remember.

"Police Academy."

Joe remembered, but his face didn't light up, no handshake, nothing. "Yeah," he said. "What can I do for you?"

Dave took his time explaining, feeling very uncomfortable as he noted that the color gradually left Joe's face, making the hardness even more noticeable.

❧

DAVE HAD NEVER SEEN anybody's face turn green before; he'd heard about it, but he'd never actually seen it. At the morgue Joe's face turned green. Then—after all, he was a police officer—he made the identification positive.

Joe obviously needed a drink, so Dave took him to

an alley speak where there was a back room for special customers, such as members of the CPD. Joe thirstily gulped down a big shot of Canadian whisky—only the best for the CPD.

"If it's murder, Joe," said Dave, "it's my case."

"If it's murder," said Joe, "let me know."

Joe left shortly after that, insisting on grabbing a city bus back for the Northwest Precinct. Although his face had turned green, he hadn't changed expression.

Dave felt vaguely worried about Joe. How could a man change so much? Happy Paisano? He'd never been exposed before to a more obviously unhappy man.

◄§

Dave carefully read the coroner's final report, with its many notations by Sluggo. And Sluggo's final notation was:

> We handle this case as murder till we are satisfied it is not. It may be suicide, and then somebody got scared and put her in the water (narcotics). She could have deliberately been given an overdose. There are many angles. Study report carefully, then write out your feelings for the file. But proceed for now as if it's murder.

Typical. "Write out your feelings . . ." Sluggo was bugs on the subject of filing reports. Downtown was buried in paper. The guys spent more time writing out stupid reports than working in the field. The truth of the matter was that Dave didn't like this case; he didn't like it at all.

6

But before he did anything else, such as writing out his feelings, he phoned Joe at Northwest Precinct and explained the whole matter to him. Joe said nothing; he listened. When Dave was through, Joe said: "Well, keep me informed," and abruptly hung up.

Two days passed. Dave so far had come up with nothing. He simply could not trace Mrs. Ricordi's movements after she'd deserted Joe three years previously. Joe had put in a claim for the body, but Dave discovered there was a prior claim by Mr. and Mrs. Lars Nielsen of Milwaukee, Wisconsin.

He called Joe about it.

Joe merely said: "Okay. It's her parents. I withdraw my claim." Bang went the phone.

Dave was beginning to develop a kind of mild dislike for Sergeant Joe Ricordi. It would take a mother to love him, Dave decided.

◆⑤

JOE LIVED ALONE in a one-bedroom apartment on the near North Side, just off Rush Street. Ever since Maria had deserted him, the children had been staying with his brother Dom and his wife, who also had two children.

Dom was doing very well for himself as a table captain at Chancy's, a very fine restaurant in The Loop where the big shots of all varieties ate. There was at all times a windfall of tips that Joe could hardly believe, though he himself would never have been able to bear the onus of Dom's status, which to Joe seemed servile.

The family had never understood Dom, who had always been cheerful, good-natured, and humble in a way that was absolutely unsuitable to the general aura of the Ricordi family. He'd humbly quit school and taken a job as a busboy at Chancy's. The Ricordi family could not understand that Dom had shown marked enterprise in getting a job there, a select place. To work as a busboy for nearly three years? The rest of the Ricordis considered Dom a bum. And they couldn't understand his elation at being accepted as a waiter, with full status. A waiter? For God's sake—so what? But now he was a slick and smooth table captain, in his tux, with an air of sophistication that was also alien to the Ricordi spirit. But how could you argue with Dom now? He was making more money than any of them, and had his sights finally on the most gilded job of all, maître d'—a position where the right kind of man could, over the years, pile up a small fortune.

Dom cheerfully accepted the burden of Joe's children, as did his wife Paula, a cheerful "mama" type, the perfect wife for Dom. Nothing bothered either of them. They took life in stride, expecting it to be full of trouble and strife, just as they expected little of children except strife and trouble. They were well adjusted to life and happy in a way that most people were not. Dom furnished everything needed and Mama Paula took care of the domestic problems as if they were nothing at all. At times both of them irritated the hell out of Joe, and this was augmented by twinges of jealousy in regard to his kids, Joe and Maria.

Wouldn't one think they would miss their father, their mother? They did not. They were happy as larks with Dom and Paula and their two young daughters, Sophia and Monica. The four of them were close in age and had a wonderful time together, off to school à la quartet, always somebody to talk to, to play with. . . . Sometimes Joe, on a visit to Dom's, had the feeling that the kids were wishing he'd go the hell home so they could have some fun.

Joe's presence seemed to inhibit everybody. Joe was serious about everything. For him, life had always been a tough proposition. Dom and Paula were serious about nothing except the Catholic religion and the kids. Joe looked grim and formidable (though he was not aware of this) and seemed to bring headquarters and crime with him into Dom's happy big apartment, Dom's happy domain. He was no fun, as Paula sometimes complained to Dom.

So . . . here was Joe, alone in his little flat, surrounded by the meager debris of his life, old pictures he'd kept from high school days, days at the Police Academy, visits to the Dunes—and dozens of snapshots of his wife Maria, now carefully put away in a drawer . . . and there was even the old accordion he used to play when he was the Happy Paisano at the Police Academy, though he had not been as happy then as he had seemed—largely because of girl trouble, but he had kept his mouth shut about that. Girls had given Joe a bad time. He was inclined to be romantic, and to many of the girls this seemed funny. They took advantage of Joe and his romanticism.

And now even the meager life of the three empty years was ruined. He'd always hoped that someday Maria would come back. Now Maria was in a drawer in the morgue—or rather Maria was now on her way by train to Milwaukee, where her parents, who had never approved of Joe, would bury her in state, in a funeral which Joe could not view, as he knew that he would not be welcome and that if he insisted on appearing, Maria's parents would no doubt come out in the open with the feelings they had largely masked while Maria was alive.

To them there was no "Maria" at all. There was only Helga, which was her true name. She'd changed it to please Joe, who kept stumbling over what to him seemed like an unnecessarily barbarous and foreign cognomen. Helga Nielsen—a blond Dane, the last person in the world Joe had expected to marry. And now he had a blond, blue-eyed daughter, Maria, who looked incongruously different from her own black-eyed, black-haired brother, Joe, Jr.

Joe, Sr. didn't know what to do with himself. When hope blows up in your face, what recourse do you have? The days at the station weren't so bad. There was always something to do—too much, if anything: an endless treadmill of misdemeanors and crimes entailing endless reams of paper and typewriter ribbons and endless man-hours of patient investigation—and never any end in sight. On the contrary, every year things got worse. It was tough trying to keep any kind of perspective. If you were not careful the world would become, in your imagination, a vast, dirty pigsty of drugs, prostitution, rape, kidnapping, armed robbery, morals offenses, drunkenness, murder, thievery, child abuse, wife beating.... The list went on and on, day after day, week after week, month after month, year after year. Hopeless. . . .

And yet it kept Joe from thinking about anything but the work at hand. But in the still of the night, within his own four walls, his troubles, his problems would rush at him full tilt . . . always Helga-Maria. And now . . . no more. Emptiness. . . .

He'd never forget the first day he saw her. She'd

come to apply for the job of policewoman. She was so good-looking all the policemen thought she was kidding. But there had been an article in the paper about it—"CPD needs help from the girls"—a silly article some crime reporter had dreamed up while he was waiting for something to happen. There'd been vague talk of increasing the number of women on the force for some time, but there was no urgency, as the article had implied, certainly no concerted attempt to recruit. But Helga had taken the article seriously and just wouldn't be put off. She was turned over to a Sergeant Spinks, now no longer among the living, who had turned her over to Joe for the paperwork. Joe helped her fill out the application. Helga Nielsen: born, Milwaukee, Wisconsin; education, high school, three semesters college; now employed as secretary-receptionist for a Chicago insurance company.

The application was turned over to the proper authorities, and Helga was called in for an interview. Joe did the calling and was present at the interview. That she would not get the job was a foregone conclusion. Aside from having no special qualifications, she was, as Sergeant Spinks said, "so damned good-looking she'd get herself in nothing but trouble, not to mention putting a lot of squad-room bulls into heat."

She got the "you will hear from us" routine. Joe was upset by the whole runaround and walked through the building with Helga and out onto the front pavement, noting the looks she was getting. It was her blond freshness that seemed to be noted by all, her straight carriage, her happy air, her aura, as if she'd just come down from a ski lodge or up from a sunny beach. It wasn't that she was beautiful in any conventional sense. It was the total picture—carriage, walk, blondness, attitude—that turned male heads.

She thanked Joe for his trouble and asked him if he thought she had a chance for the job. Joe didn't know what to say. Of course she didn't. But why tell her so at this point? Maybe her desire to be a policewoman —of all things—would wear off, nullifying the disappointment.

"I'm not really sure," said Joe.

He was very reluctant to let her go. If he did he'd probably never see her again. Taking his courage in his hands, he asked: "Could I see you sometime?"

"Why not?" asked Helga; then she gave him the phone number at her apartment. "I always did want to get to know a policeman. They must lead very adventurous lives."

A foolish girl, what else? Joe's mind told him, but mind had nothing to do with it.

So began Joe's pleasant nightmare with Helga Nielsen, who was so different from any of the Italian girls Joe had known—and he'd known nothing else— that he could never figure out where he stood or what was expected of him. Helga completely baffled him. She was absolutely forthright in everything, much to Joe's embarrassment at times. She went to bed with Joe as if it were all a matter of course. Joe couldn't believe it and stumbled around in a daze, wondering if he were dreaming.

All the Ricordis thought he was out of his mind, although they liked Helga in spite of everything . . . everybody did. What was there to dislike? They might laugh at her. To them, she seemed awfully foolish and naive at times, yet extremely likable she always remained. But for Joe's wife . . . ? Ridiculous! Joe needed a good Italian girl who understood what life was all about—and was not foolish like Helga but practical, and would know how to raise Joe's children and manage the money.

But Joe had a very hard time persuading Helga to marry him. "It will spoil everything," she kept insisting, but Joe broke her down. Or rather what was really true: Helga couldn't stand Joe's obvious unhappiness. It was all he thought about: getting married. Joe was conventional; Helga was not. The relationship did not distress her at all. But distress Joe it did, not only because he was Catholic-raised, but because he had an inborn sense of fitness. "Living in sin" was just not Joe's idea of happiness.

So finally they were married, and Helga took Joe to Milwaukee to meet her parents. They ran a small but prosperous Danish restaurant and bakery, and worked from morning till night. They simply could not understand why Helga had married an Italian police officer from that wicked Sodom of the south, Chicago. They were coldly polite, tight-lipped, Old World–types who reminded Joe of some of the Old World–Italian types he'd known—carrying Europe to America with them and disapproving of everything that didn't remind them of their former homeland.

On the way back Helga laughed about it. "They found you shocking, Joe," she said. But Joe did not find it at all funny. He felt hurt and humiliated.

And so the years passed and the children came, and Helga became Maria and tried to manage things as a "good Italian girl" would have managed them, and Joe worked hard and scarcely knew that other women existed. Maria was all the woman he wanted or ever would want. As for Maria, to him she seemed completely contented. And he noted with pleasure, as the years passed, that she just did not seem to age. At thirty her figure was the same as at twenty-five, while many of the Italian girls Joe had known were now fat and looking ten years older than their actual ages. Nor did he miss the envious, unfriendly glances cast in her direction by many of the Italian girls.

She got along best with Dom and Paula; the three of them were always laughing together and telling jokes, and one day Dom said to Paula, "If I ever turn up missing, you'll know I've run off with Maria." It was a joke, of course, and Paula took it as such, and yet Dom hadn't been entirely joking.

And so Joe Ricordi found seven years of happiness, as things go in this world: it wasn't perfect; there were occasional arguments, children's illnesses, money trouble . . . but nothing really serious to mar Joe's satisfaction with life. Toward the end Joe noticed that Maria seemed to be away from home a lot and that sometimes she was late picking up the children from Dom's, where they loved to stay and play. But in the evening, at night, she was always there, as she'd been for seven years. And besides, Joe had complete trust in her, as in all his life he had never trusted a single person before, even members of his own family.

And then one day Maria took the children to Dom's and never returned to pick them up. A boy delivered a note, which the manager of the apartment house where Joe then lived brought up to him. Joe still had it in his wallet, wrapped in cellophane and tightly sealed.

It read:

Dear Joe:
I didn't want to do this but I couldn't stand it any longer. I did not want to get married in the

first place. I am all right. Don't worry about me
and don't look for me.

Love,
Helga

The signature was the clincher. She was no longer
"Maria." She was Helga once again. Worry about her
he did. Look for her he did not. Well . . . he'd finally
found her!

෫

IT WAS SUMMER and a very hot night. But Ted Beck was
sweating from things other than the heat. Ted was a
large man, nearly forty, with blond Swedish good
looks, though he was not a Swede but a Pole, born
Taddeus Byscznski. Willie Pons, his weird factotum,
was trying to soothe him.

"But Ted, I can't blast him if I can't find him. He
lammed, back to Detroit or God knows where. He
knew you'd have his hide for this."

" 'Weight her,' I told him," said Ted. "I made it
strong. 'Weight her,' I said. I thought he understood
me."

"Oh, he understood you all right," said Willie, "and
if I can find him I'll cool him. He must have panicked
for some reason. He'd have more brains than to slough
this off . . ."

"I'm the one who panicked," cried Ted. "Why did
I do it? Was I crazy? So she died. People die every day.
Why didn't I just give her a funeral, like anybody
else?"

Willie said nothing. He was sure Ted would answer
himself in a moment.

"Goddamn it, Willie," cried Ted, "why didn't you stop me?"

"Because you were doing the right thing. It was that creep Layton who bungled it—not you. If she just disappeared, fine. Who would know? But once we get the police in it . . ."

"Who's got the case?"

"Dave Santorelli."

"Is there any chance that we could . . . ?"

"No," said Willie. "Downtown. Maheny. And I'll remind you, Murtaugh may get into it if anything is turned up, if you know what I mean."

Ted was so nervous he could hardly light his cigar. Finally he managed it. "That damned woman," he said. "Nothing but trouble, trouble, ever since the first day I met her. There I was, minding my own business at Gabel's, having my lunch—and she comes in and sits just across from me at a little corner table. A blond whizzer . . ."

Willie didn't want to hear about it. It was all so stupid, always had been: Ted making a jackass of himself over a broad who was at least thirty-two or -three years old. At first Willie had thought she was just a new recruit for a certain type of trade. Blondes were very big with certain segments of the population. But no—nothing like that. Ted had finally found himself a private woman, much to his taste, stopping the usual parade in and out of his apartment of "prospects." Now the "prospects" had been shunted off to Willie and his helpers, like that big idiot Red Layton, who couldn't even do a simple thing like weighting a body so it wouldn't rise.

How the blonde got on the junk Willie never knew. Not through Ted, that was for sure. Ted abhorred junk. Earlier, he'd had some very bad experiences with junkies, one of the episodes landing him in the Cook County jail for a short stretch. Maybe she'd picked up the habit on one of her various run-outs— the disappearances that had driven Ted frantic. Willie often wondered just what that Helga broad had had that was so special!

Ted had risen and was pacing the floor when the phone rang. Willie answered it; then after a moment he turned and looked at Ted. "Okay," said Willie, "I'll tell him."

"What was that?" asked Ted apprehensively.

"Trouble," said Willie. "Bones."

Ted gave a kind of groan and sank back into his chair. Bones was William Macready, M-6's lawyer and second. M-6 was the prostitution boss of the whole Southwest area, answerable to nobody except The Man in Cicero. Ted did not even know who M-6 was. He knew only the men who collected for M-6, and M-6's lawyer, the thin gentleman with his Old World charm, Bones.

"You mean they've found out something already?"

"Could be. Bones wants you at his place in an hour."

"Did he say why?"

"No," said Willie. "But it's not hard to figure."

Ted had to restrain a sudden panicked desire to flee, as apparently Red Layton had done when it hit the papers that Helga's body had been discovered. But he gradually steadied himself. Reprimands he could stand—even rough ones—and Bones, in spite of his gentlemanly appearance, could be very rough at times. That's all it amounted to, Ted kept telling himself: just a reprimand. Nothing but a reprimand.

Ted poured himself a drink and stood in the middle

of the big living room, looking about him at the elegance. He'd come a long way from the Stockyards, a very long way. His secret fear was that suddenly he'd be deprived of all he'd won.

❦

JOE WAS HOME again, and the interminable hours ground on. The evenings, the nights now seemed endless. He took pleasure in nothing. Once he'd liked to bowl, to have a few drinks with the guys at the corner, to go see a movie, but even these simple pleasures had lost their savor. So now it was from home to the station, long hours of work, then home again . . . to emptiness, to hours that seemed to hesitate as if the clock of the universe had run down. He'd think it was nearly midnight and time to sack out, but his watch would say ten o'clock.

This evening had been a trying one. He'd gone over to Dom's to see the kids and explain to them what had happened to their mother. It had been obscure in the papers; there was no doubt talk around the neighborhood. The story was as follows: their mother had been very ill and had died accidentally. And her funeral had been held by her parents in a city a long way off and none of them could take the time to go. The kids listened but made no comment. They would no doubt discuss it among themselves later.

Well . . . at least it was something. And Joe had felt relieved in a way, except that later, while he and Dom and the missus were having a glass of wine, he'd heard the kids laughing and playing in the back of the apartment. Didn't they care? Or didn't they understand? Or what?

Joe was plagued by violent feelings. He wanted to

strike. He didn't really know what he wanted to do. One night he noted his service revolver lying on the table in its holster, and he'd suddenly had a desire to use it—maybe even on himself.

Murder or not—and that was doubtful—it was all the same as far as Joe was concerned. The thought of Maria being callously dumped into the river enraged him. And the thought kept returning, making peace of mind utterly impossible. Even in the middle of complicated work at the station, the thought would come to him and he'd wince from the pictures that rose before his mind. The brutal indignity!

Joe glanced at his watch. Nine o'clock—and interminable hours ahead till the alarm clock sounded the clarion call of a new day. It was a very hot night. All his windows were open, but no breeze was coming in. The night seemed almost airless, like an old attic. On his way home he'd seen people sitting out on fire escapes and on the front steps of the apartment buildings. In midsummer in Chicago when there was an offshore wind, the heat was all but unbearable. But Joe had never been so conscious of it before. In his present state of mind, he was now vulnerable to everything. What would he do with himself in the long years ahead? What could he ever do?

There was a light tapping at his door. It was Dave Santorelli, and he smiled rather apologetically as Joe let him in. Joe's grim face showed nothing, but actually Joe was feeling a kind of relief. At least the big guy from Downtown would break the monotony for a little while.

They sat, and Joe poured out a couple of glasses of wine. "They call it Chianti," said Joe. "It's rough, but it's not so bad."

"Joe," said Dave, sipping the wine, "I hate to bother

you, but I'm getting noplace. Have you got a picture
I could use?"

Joe hesitated. Yes, he had pictures, many pictures,
but the idea of having them passed around . . . He
thought it over for a long time, saying nothing. Dave
waited. Dave was a very patient man, especially when
he was on a case. He had outwaited many a guy, to the
guy's detriment. Finally Joe got up, went to a drawer,
and returned with a blown-up snapshot, a rather large
picture of a tall, smiling blond woman in a short-
skirted dress, a scarf blowing in the wind. It had been
taken at a beach, and Dave could see the shadow of
whoever had taken the picture. It was an inept ama-
teur job, but effective and plain—a true, good, identifi-
able picture of a subject. Dave was surprised at what
a striking woman Mrs. Ricordi had been. No Italian,
that was for sure. A Swede, maybe.

"That one is the most like her," said Joe. "It's okay.
I've got the negative."

"We can duplicate this," said Dave. "It ought to
help. I've got three men out now, Joe. Nothing so far."

Joe just sat and stared.

"Could I ask you a few questions?" asked Dave.

"Sure. Why not?"

Dave hesitated and scratched his head. Joe made
him very uncomfortable. He seemed tense, tough,
hard, far away—hardly more animate than a piece of
furniture.

"Was there trouble between you?" asked Dave.

Joe merely looked at him, his eyes hard as stones.

"I'm only trying to do my job, Joe."

"There was never any trouble between us—never,"
said Joe.

"Then why did she go away?"

"I don't know," said Joe. "I never did understand it. She was a fine wife and mother . . . and one day she just went away."

"Did she ever communicate with you after she left?"

"No," said Joe. "She left a note, that's all."

Dave felt more and more uncomfortable as Joe fidgeted and seemed ready to fly off his chair.

"Did you know all her friends?"

"Friends? Yeah, sure. But we didn't have many—just people you say hello to. Our friends were mostly family."

Dave squirmed but finally brought it out. "So . . . you never had any suspicions that she was seeing somebody else on the side?"

"She couldn't have been," said Joe. "She was always home."

Joe was lying. But he didn't care. The hell with it. He'd finally noted the long absences, the lateness—in the daytime—but had made nothing of it then. Now it was clear. But should he accuse his dead wife . . . ?

"It would make it easier, Joe," said Dave, "if we could get a line on whoever it was she went away with. It doesn't make sense that she'd just walk out of her home for no good reason."

"Women get funny ideas sometimes, you know," said Joe. "They get a little nutty, like. I don't mean crazy. But . . . well, strange ideas, like. . . ."

Dave could see he was going to get no place with Joe. And it was understandable. No man liked to admit that his wife had simply walked out on him because she'd found a man she liked better. If that were not the case here, what was? It was the only thing that made sense.

Dave finished his wine and got up. "This picture

should be a big help, Joe," he said. "And you know we're going to do our best."

"Right," said Joe.

At the door they shook hands rather awkwardly, then Dave left. Joe stood lost in thought for a long time; then he got all the snapshots out of the drawer, spread them out on the desk, and slowly studied them . . . reliving his happy past with Helga-Maria, as Chicago sweltered in its first heat wave of the season.

▪§

William "Bones" Macready was conservative in everything but morality, in clothes, in women, in manner of living, in practically anything else you could name, so M-6's life-style always seemed to him like an affront to the human race.

Bones was six feet one and hardly ever broke the scales at more than a hundred and forty pounds. He was cadaverously elegant, always well barbered and manicured, his shoes always with a high polish. He wore only dark suits, white shirts, conservatively patterned ties—and he lived in a conservatively "exclusive" apartment-hotel with a uniformed doorman out in front.

He was a member of the bar, but his activities were mostly extralegal. He was expert at hiding money from the Internal Revenue Service and at hiring just the right lawyers for special cases. Without Bones, the M-6 organization couldn't operate. And yet he knew that M-6's ego would never admit that he was invaluable. Bones took it in stride, especially as from time to time he noted the size of the bankroll he was accumulating. Also he was aware that the crowned head lies uneasy. M-6—money, power and all—was a mere front, a straw man for The Man in Cicero, who really called the turns. M-6 was dispensable. Bones, in actual fact, was not. Who could replace him? But Bones did not want to be put out in front. He wanted a guy like M-6—Mario Fanelli—between him and the real power. No matter what happened, Mario was responsible—that was his job.

Now let's get back to Mario Fanelli's life-style. He lived in a penthouse at the top of a newly built apartment-hotel on the Gold Coast. Its decor, as Bones thought to himself, was old Paris whorehouse, with lots of red and gold and glitter, and from the ceiling was suspended a fractured glass ball, as in a dance hall, that gave off strange glitterings and patterns of light when it moved slowly in the breeze. Mario was either dressed to the teeth, according to his lights, loud colors predominating—or sitting around in his undershirt and sock feet.

Mario was tall, heavy, and running to fat, with a receding hairline surrounded by thick, curly, black hair. His face was fattish, his features undistinguished. His eyes were small, dark, pouched, and cunning. He sweated a lot and kept mopping his face, and today he was sweating even more than usual, as the city sweltered with not even the breath of a breeze at penthouse level, though the windows were all open.

Mario's taste in women went with the decor of the apartment. They all looked like Jean Harlow, one replacement following another. M-6's men would spot one—"There's M-6's type," they'd say—and she'd be put aside for his approval. Many were called; few were called upon to serve. Mario suffered from long stretches of indifference, which manifested itself in a tendency toward celibacy—the result, no doubt, of satiation.

No one was close to Mario. He had not wife, child, or friend. He had only broads and employees. As for his family, no one knew where he'd come from—the speculation ranged from Italy to Brooklyn. But he had no accent at all, so he couldn't have come from Italy. Nor did he talk Brooklynese. If anything, he talked Chicagoese. Mario's origins were a mystery.

Today he was in his undershirt—pale blue silk—and socks, clocked.

He sat with his big feet up on a grotesquely carved coffee table, smoking a cigar and sweating as Bones gave him the tale, which was not a happy one. Occasionally he grunted.

"Willie kept me informed," Bones was saying. "But I didn't think it was anything very serious. Ted fell all apart over this woman. But . . . he's entitled to a private life. . . ."

"Yuh," grunted Mario.

"The thing is, we didn't know who she was. We didn't know she was a copper's wife and neither did Ted, I'm sure. He picked her up in a restaurant. It turned into something and she left home. . . ."

"Who's Willie?" asked Mario, a step or two behind.

"Willie Pons. A hundred percent," said Bones. "His real name is Ponchielli. He keeps an eye on things."

"Oke," said Mario.

"Well, here's the problem. If the case could be switched to the jurisdiction of the Southwest Precinct . . ."

"So get it switched."

"It's not that easy. The body was found in the jurisdiction of the Downtown Precinct. And you know about that. Maheny. Murtaugh . . ."

"Get it switched," said Mario wearily. "Put the screws to Krumpacker."

"We don't own the captain, you know."

"No? For that kind of dough?"

"He owns us."

Mario grunted slightly, then asked, as if Bones had lost him, "So . . . what's the big problem?"

"The big problem is, if they trace her to Ted, it may get a little complicated. Sometimes the cops get crazy and vag people. And what means of support could Ted show? He runs the whorehouses, right? It's against the law. Right?"

"If they want to get silly," said Mario indifferently. "I still don't get the problem."

"Well, there is more than one. The guy that dumped her was supposed to weight her down. He didn't. So now he's taken a run-out—and if the Downtown boys ever get their hands on him . . ."

"So why is he alive?"

"He's alive," said Bones, "because Willie can't find him."

"So find him," said Mario. "And about that Ted—maybe he has to go too. This kind of louse-up is no good."

Mario mopped his head with a big silk handkerchief and groaned. "This damned heat's killing me," he said. "I wish somebody would turn it off."

"That's something we can't fix," said Bones.

Mario laughed, then mopped his head again. The glass ball gave off weird reflections—the red and gold furniture glittered—and Bones, as usual, felt contaminated.

TED WAS VERY IMPATIENT for Willie to get there. Willie hadn't wanted to talk over the phone, but he had intimated that the news was good, very good. Ted had had the shakes ever since the cold, blunt, probing interview with Bones, who really gave him the creeps. He had once heard Bones referred to as a "good embalming job," and that just about covered it, in Ted's opinion. Bones seemed inhuman, immune to the stresses and strains of normal life. He didn't even seem to sweat on the hottest days, such as now. During the interview Ted had felt wilted, with his shirt sticking to his back, but Bones had seemed cool as a cucumber, almost like a department-store dummy, in his dark suit with the vest, across which was stretched a very expensive platinum watch chain that glittered hypnotically. From Bones you could expect neither mercy nor understanding. Ted hadn't slept well since.

Finally Willie arrived, and the news was definitely good.

"We've got him," said Willie. "And this one I handle personally." Then he took a slip of paper from his pocket and gave it to Ted. "We've got to take care of this broad. She set him up. Smart, right? She was with us before, but she got in trouble with Geraldine over on Devonshire, and Geraldine kicked her out. She's been working call, trying to free-lance with some two-bit pimp she knows. We put her back in—but not with Geraldine. All right? And I slipped her a C—and you can now slip it back to me."

Ted, feeling younger and lighter, took out his wallet, handed Willie a bill, and then put the slip of paper in the wallet.

"I'll take care of her. What's she like?"

"Good-looking young redhead," said Willie. "She's okay, take my word for it."

"Fine. So?"

"So . . . I'll call you later. I'm waiting for Pete. He's getting the car fixed."

Ted felt like celebrating. He showered, shaved, put on fresh clothes, and went out to Gabel's for dinner, where he had turtle soup with sherry, filet mignon with bearnaise, pommes soufflées, and cheese and fruit, then black coffee.

It was very seldom now that he remembered the want of the past, the dinners of bread and soup, the greasy spoons where he'd eaten when he worked as a mechanic and before he was lucky enough to get that job chauffeuring—the job that had put him on the right track—and here he was! And as he ate, he wondered vaguely about that crazy woman, Helga. A policeman's wife? Incredible! And what had she been doing in Gabel's, a real swank place . . . ? "Living, for a change," Helga had told him, when asked (not that he'd known she was a policeman's wife or anybody's wife). But her clothes just hadn't seemed appropriate to Gabel's; they weren't expensive enough—and Ted knew a lot about clothes. It was part of the business.

Ted remembered Helga with regret. But he was glad it was all over. She had been a great puzzle to him. Although she didn't look it, she was flighty and unpredictable. You never knew what she'd come up with. And every time they had a serious quarrel, she would disappear—once for nearly three months. When she came back, she was on the junk, and from then on Ted had been forced to see that she had her supply, in spite of his hatred for drugs in any form. Was it the result, again, of "living, for a change"? Helga was very experimental. She always wanted to try things. And she was always full of what to Ted were silly ideas. She never seemed to see things straight. There was always a Helga-version that startled him with its difference from his own version of whatever it was: Helga was a kook, what else?

In death she remained a mystery to him, a complete mystery. How could she have been married to a city police officer for seven years and raised two kids? Ted simply could not make himself believe it, and yet apparently it was true.

"How was your dinner, Mr. Beck?" asked the maître d'.

"Fine, as usual," said Ted, smiling.

❧

RED LAYTON sat listening to the radio and congratulating himself. The perfect spot to hide away, Vera's little flat by the river. It was even ten degrees cooler here. It was a kind of motel, low and long, with two stories and an open balcony that ran the length of the building—and just beyond was the river. Red's two windows were wide open, and occasionally a dampish breeze wafted in.

Vera had turned the place over to him, with the rent paid up till the end of the month. Vera was lighting out for St. Louis, she'd told him, where money was loose and there was not so much competition.

Well . . . the end of the month was a long way off, according to Red's style of reckoning—ordinarily he lived just from day to day, and when the end of the month came around . . . then he'd make up his mind what to do. He was positive Willie would figure he'd

28

lit out for home—Detroit. Even so, it was just as well to hole up till the heat was off, as Red was sure it would be eventually.

If they were looking for him at all, they were looking in all the usual places. And this was a very unusual place indeed—a neighborhood entirely unknown to Red, and no doubt to Willie and the boys.

"So I blew it," thought Red.

He'd got into an argument with Pete and another guy, about what he couldn't remember now, and as a result of a hot head, he'd gone off without the weights and the rope. He hadn't discovered this till he got to the river, and he'd made up his mind he'd be damned if he'd drive all the way back with that body in the car. All he needed was a traffic accident! So he'd tried to rig something up hastily, and it hadn't worked. He'd blown it.

Good music was coming over the radio, jazz music, the kind Red liked. His shoulders moved slightly in time, his head following suit, then his foot began to tap. Suddenly there were two blasts from the open window and Red pitched forward out of his chair and slowly stretched out his full length on the floor.

Willie climbed quickly in the window, observed Red for a moment, then frisked him and took out his wallet. Red had quite a bit of money in fairly large bills. Willie took the money out and threw the empty wallet on the floor. Then as an afterthought he tossed a five-dollar bill down beside Red, as if a robber had left it in his panicked flight.

Willie climbed back out the window, then paused, looking all around him. Nothing. So he leisurely descended the stairs, went out through the back, and down a short stone stairway to an alley where Pete was waiting with the car. At the far end of the alley gleamed the black river, reflecting the shore lights.

"Jesus, that was loud," said Pete as Willie got in and they drove off.

"Look at the dough," said Willie. "Here, I'll split it."

Pete put his share away, laughing.

"Red got killed and robbed, what else?" said Willie, taking off his gloves.

"Yeah," said Pete. "Red always was careless with money."

◄§

AND so Red Layton finally appeared in the Downtown morgue, where his body lay unclaimed. His death had not gone unnoted. It was already in the hands of a be-deviled homicide man from Downtown, and even Mur-taugh, of the Metropolitan Hoodlum Squad, had been apprised of it. Maybe Red had been killed for his money and maybe he hadn't—but how could you prove anything one way or another, without a witness?

To the police, another hoodlum with a long record had bitten the dust and there were no tears shed; but the homicide man from Downtown went conscien-tiously about his job, yet with little hope of bringing anybody to book. In 1927, the year before, 350-odd hoods had bitten the dust, and with only one murder conviction as a result.

◄§

THE NEWS was relayed to Bones, and Bones dropped by to see Mario, who this evening was all dressed up in a white evening tux with a maroon cummerbund, a pink shirt, and a dark red bow tie.

"Willie managed it," Bones explained as he sipped a liqueur with Mario, who was "having some broads in for a late supper" and asked Bones to remain—but Bones pled heavy work. The "broads" Mario was having in were from the chorus of a road-company show from Broadway, and it promised to be quite a night.

"The Man might even drop in," said Mario. "He saw the show and liked it."

The Man was always being expected to drop in, but he never did.

"Fine, fine," said Bones.

"So . . . now that problem's taken care of. What about Beck?"

"He's a good man," said Bones.

"No," said Mario. "Good men don't cause beefs like this. So what do you think?"

"We need him—till word comes through otherwise."

"You mean the beef may cool . . . ?"

"Yes."

Mario stroked his chin for a long time. "Well . . ." he said, finally. "Maybe I'll sleep on it. Who could we move up?"

"I don't know of anybody," said Bones.

"There's always somebody."

"Such as they are."

"All right," said Mario. "I'll have my party—and then I'll sleep on it."

Later Bones stood looking out a corridor window at the lake and the curving arm of the shore, with its huge lineup of hotels and apartment complexes. A summer moon was showing—a hot-looking moon to match the weather. Lights gleamed all along the shore. Finally the elevator arrived (there was a private one to the penthouse from this floor, then you had to wait). It was empty except for an attendant in a sharp-looking semi-military uniform.

As the elevator descended, Bones thought: "In this place they ought to dress the help as Bedouins or Zouaves or something like that. Veiled belly dancers would be nice, too . . . on the mezzanine. I think I'll suggest it to Mario."

Bones kept laughing to himself as he crossed the grotesquely elegant lobby toward the taxi stand.

◆§

Joe looked up from his work to find a well-dressed man smiling at him from the doorway, a vaguely familiar man—and with a start he finally recognized him: Cy Travis, who used to ride a chair in the press room far back in time when Joe had been a rookie at Downtown.

"Hi, Joe," said Cy, advancing with outstretched hand. His pleasure at the sight of Joe seemed excessive —at least to Joe—but it was to be expected, thought Joe, as he rose and negligently shook hands. Cy was now a "politician," administrative assistant to Alderman Hruba, who more or less bossed the Southwest Side Aldermanic District—not only administrative assistant, but PR man . . . so naturally it was friendly smiles and handshakes all around, part of the trade.

Cy took a seat beside Joe's desk, carefully pulled up his trousers to preserve the crease, crossed his legs, took out a gold cigarette case, and they lit up. They'd been friends, in a way, in the old Downtown days, as

near as two such disparate individuals could be: Cy
from well-to-do folks in Ohio, a college graduate, and
Joe from the fringes of Little Italy, who had barely
finished high school and who to Cy seemed Italian—
that is, "foreign"—to his fingertips.

Cy's name had always amused Joe. Cy was a hayseed
name to Joe. In those days most men carried pocket
watches—wristwatches were still considered rather
sissy, though they'd now risen higher in the scale because of their acceptance by soldiers in World War I.
Older men, like Bones, still carried watches and dis-
dained the wristwatch. Well . . . Joe had made some
crack about Cy's name and Cy had taken out his gold
watch and shown Joe the engraving on the back:
"Cyrus D. Travis III—a gift from his loving parents."
Laughing, Joe had promptly taken out his beat-up old
"railroad" watch, a gift from his "loving" grandfather,
and with a nail file had scratched on the back: "Joseph
Ricordi I."

For a while Cy had been the butt of jokes around
Downtown, the older reporters calling him "fresh
fish," but Cy had never turned a hair. He was a smart
boy; it had been recognized from the first—too smart,
maybe, to spend the rest of his life as an ink-stained
wretch, so he'd taken the political pathway and was at
present doing very well. There was a definite aura of
success—even, perhaps, of self-satisfaction—about
him.

"I was over this way," said Cy, "and I just thought
I'd drop in and say hello. I don't know what to say, Joe.
At a time like this there's really nothing I can say
except I'm sorry."

"Right," said Joe, nodding coldly. He had no feelings whatever in regard to Cy. The years had passed;

they'd drifted far apart. Actually Cy was a stranger to Joe.

"Is any progress being made?" asked Cy after a moment.

"Not so far. Haven't heard a thing."

Cy sat shaking his head. "That's too bad. Downtown! We know how it is, don't we? Too much to do. Never enough manpower. Just a matter of jurisdiction, really."

"Yeah," said Joe, wondering.

"At the Southwest it's different," said Cy. "We've got a different kind of captain—active, very active. Captain Krumpacker, you know. A real dynamo—and young. Never makes the creamed chicken and peas circuit." Cy laughed, then broke off and sat studying Joe.

And Joe just sat looking back at him. He'd heard different about Captain Krumpacker, but maybe it was only rumor. Rumors were always flying around through the CPD—there was a persistent grapevine. It was said that the whole Southwest Precinct—and Alderman Hruba—were all on the take. Was Cy also on the take? It seemed to Joe maybe there might be something funny about this.

"No leads at all?" asked Cy. "You see, all I know is what I read in the paper. I haven't read anything. Nothing."

"No leads," said Joe.

"Well," said Cy, "Santorelli is a good man, but he's worked to death. I suppose the two of you keep in touch."

"More or less, yes," said Joe.

Cy shrugged, then glanced at his wristwatch, an expensive gold one with a massive gold band. "Well, it's about that time," he said. "How about lunch?"

"Thanks just the same," said Joe. "I've got a heavy load, so I brought a sandwich."

"Can't I tempt you? Good steaks and beer at Fester's just around the corner."

"Sorry," said Joe. "Thanks."

Cy hesitated, then got to his feet. "You know, I often think about the old days at Downtown. Remember, Joe? It was fun in a way. I was fresh fish, remember? But you didn't pour it on like the others."

"I was fresh fish myself," said Joe.

"Well," said Cy, "I'm going to keep watching this case—strictly out of personal interest. If you remember, I met the charming Mrs. Ricordi once . . ."

Joe remembered now something he'd completely forgotten—the surprise in Cyrus D. Travis III's eyes when Joe had introduced Maria to him as Mrs. Ricordi. It happened in a little counter restaurant in an alleylike street behind Downtown, where the low-income group ate. They'd had a hard time shaking Cy off. They'd only been married a short time and were spending every minute together that they could squeeze out of Joe's busy schedule. To them, Cy was an interloper—a persistent one.

"Yeah," said Joe. "I remember."

Cy hesitated, then said: "To tell you the truth, Joe, I have a very strong feeling about this case. A personal feeling. It was a terrible thing. I'd appreciate it if you would keep me posted."

"Well, thanks, Cy," said Joe. "Sure, sure."

After Cy had gone, Joe sat for a long time lost in silent thought. What the hell was all this? It didn't smell right. And yet . . . what interest could Cy possibly have in it? Was he misjudging Cy? He'd always seemed like a reasonably good guy. Finally Joe shrugged it off—at least for the time being—got out his Italian sausage sandwich and his small Thermos of coffee and slowly ate his lunch, remembering Maria, who else?—and the way she'd looked that day at Harry's, with Cy staring at her, unable to disguise his surprise. This!—is Mrs. Ricordi?

ᕦ§

THE WORD was spread fast, and an hour later it was relayed to M-6—who had a hangover and to whom at the moment all the uses of this world seemed stale, flat, and unprofitable. One of Alderman Hruba's boys was a friend of Joe's. And the word had come from the horse's mouth. No leads, nothing, in regard to Mrs. Ricordi. So M-6, though at the moment he would rather have said off with his head, granted Ted Beck a reprieve.

ᕦ§

IT WAS AFTER eight o'clock and Joe was listening to the radio, trying hard to interest himself in something . . . anything! It was still hot, but not sweltering as before, as the wind had swung around and was now beginning to blow in from the lake. Occasionally he noted that his curtains billowed and that for a moment there was a welcome feeling of freshness in the air.

Just as the program he was listening to concluded, there was a tap at the door. Santorelli again? Joe hoped so, hoped he was bringing good news for a change, a lead, anything. He opened the door, fully expecting to see Santorelli, but instead, to his surprise, there stood a good-looking girl, medium-size, shapely, with a turned-up nose, a pert expression, big, heavily lashed black eyes, and thick black hair, bobbed. Obviously an "Italian-American."

"Mr. Ricordi . . . I mean, Sergeant Ricordi . . . ?" asked the girl in a slightly husky voice.

"Yes," said Joe, barring her way as it seemed to him she'd made a slight move to enter.

"Could I talk to you?"

"What about?" asked Joe coldly. Occasionally guys got set up, and he was taking no chances. Phony rape charges once they were inside, extortion, God knows what! A cop was fair game.

The girl seemed very nervous. Now she fumbled in her purse and brought out a crumpled-looking note that seemed to have been written on butcher's paper.

It read:

> Joe, this is Gina Brazzi. She's OK. You help me. I'll help you. Listen to her. I can break a certain case. Why should I go to Dave?
>
> Dago Al

Dago Al! Joe had almost forgotten—it dated back to high-school days and the days of the neighborhood youth gangs. Dago Al! Nobody could know about that except the guy himself—Giovanni Alberto, who was a big-time hood now known as Johnny Albert. In the old days Giovanni had called himself Dago Al, for laughs.

Joe motioned her in, but he left the door open. Gina noted this but made no comment.

"Well," said Joe.

It was obvious that the grim-faced Joe put Gina off,

way off. She was very nervous and for a moment could hardly organize herself to talk.

"Johnny's in—at the Northwest Precinct," she said.

"What charge?"

"Aggravated assault and battery—but he says he was bum-rapped. And we're both short of funds. You see, I'm living with Johnny now. If he could pay Melvin, Melvin could get the charge reduced and spring him. But now they got him set up with a public defender. No good."

Melvin was a very sharp criminal lawyer with a lot of clout around the courts, crooked as a dog's hind leg, but in his branch of the profession, that was an absolute necessity.

"Johnny's paid Melvin a lot of money over the years," said Gina, "but now when he needs him . . ."

"How much?" asked Joe.

"A thousand dollars, and I've managed to get up five hundred of it," said Gina.

Joe read the note over again, and now there was hope in his heart for the first time since Dave Santorelli had brought him the bad news that day at the station. Johnny was just the kind of guy who might know something.

Suddenly Joe made up his mind. "All right. Now here's what you tell him. As soon as he's sprung, he's to call me—in my office—and we'll set up a meeting. And you tell Giovanni if there is anything phony about this—if he runs out—I'll have his hide no matter what."

Gina stared at Joe big-eyed, her lashes quivering. "But he said you were an old pal of his!"

"I was. But what's that got to do with it? If he is pulling a fast one on me, it may be his last. You tell him that."

"I'll tell him, I'll tell him," said pretty Gina nervously.

"Now step outside," said Joe.

Gina glanced at Joe, puzzled, then did as she was told. Joe shut the door in her face, crossed to an old desk against a wall, turned it around, and extracted a thick wallet from the back. Although Joe had a checking account and a savings account, both rather small, he kept his reserve in the house. It was something he'd learned from his father. When suddenly you need money, what do you do if the banks are closed and there is no place to cash a check? This little matter would deplete his reserve, but it might—it just might —be worth it.

Joe opened the door and counted out the money to Gina. "And don't forget," he warned.

He scared Gina. She stared at him with her big eyes dark as ripe olives, her lashes fluttering; then she turned and hurried out.

Later she said to Johnny, "That old pal of yours, Joe Ricordi, is certainly a tough bastard. He seems more like a hood than a cop."

Big Johnny laughed loudly. "Joe? Naw, naw. Joe's no tough bastard. It's just his way."

Joe stood at his open window looking down into the street. It was cooling off fast, and he felt the tension leaving him. Maybe now he could get a good night's sleep for a change.

ڡج

AND WHILE Joe paced the floor, alternately hopeful and suspicious of Johnny Albert and his intentions, and while Ted Beck, having a drink at Wally's Piano Bar and listening to the singing of the dazzling brunette at the piano, was beginning to wonder if his sense of present safety was not perhaps exaggerated, and while Willie Pons, Pete Daley, and a couple of their friends were wrangling over a card game, and while Dave Santorelli was arguing with the teens about their going to summer school (their final report cards being "disgraceful," as he put it), and while Red Layton lay dead to the world in a drawer in the morgue . . . Bones was engaged in an activity of his own.

It was an activity far different from those of the others and in a milieu where nobody had ever heard William Macready called Bones. He was attending an outdoor cocktail party on the terrace of the Edgewater Beach Hotel, a party given as a kind of kickoff for the opera season that began in mid-September at the Chicago Civic. William Macready was a donor, and his name was always listed in the opera programs.

When he appeared, a blond lady of ample proportions cried: "Oh—there's William."

Bones was William to these people, a prosperous lawyer of impeccable taste and a very eligible bachelor indeed, though he was pushing fifty. There was something about his former wife . . . wasn't there? Hadn't she been put away? Nobody was quite sure, though it was said that he had refused to divorce her for nearly twenty years. Very little seemed to be known about William, except that now he was a widower at long last, and quite a few ladies of this set, widowed themselves, looked very kindly on William and hoped to throw the net over him.

Even William had had a cross to bear. His rich wife had turned out to be an alcoholic—there always seemed to be a thorn among the roses—and William had put up with shocking things in order to preserve his status (as the son-in-law of Beggs Inc., as some facetiously said) and retain his blood contact with the most prestigious brokerage firm in the Chicago area. Adeline had been palmed off on him by the Beggs family, no doubt about it, and William had not had a single warning. He had never seen Adeline take a drink before marriage, and the first time he came home and found her on the floor he'd thought she was dead. . . . Oh, well, water over the dam and beer over the bar. . . .

"Yes, yes," cried the buxom lady, "there's William."

Smiling, William crossed over to them, and they stood at the railing talking and looking out across the moonlit water. A welcome lake breeze caressed their faces as the reflected lights from a hundred windows danced on the water and a string orchestra played, and later one of the local divas sang. She was rather hefty, and the flowers on her bosom kept rising and falling as if from barometric pressure, and William stood listening and wondering why she didn't stop eating so much and get some of that avoirdupois off. One opera singer explained to William that the weight helped her "project." And he was tempted to say, "So I notice"—but William was never the one to say the wrong thing at the wrong time; he'd built a whole career on refraining.

"It's *Carmen* for opening night," said the large blond lady to William. "I love *Carmen*, don't you?"

"Oh, yes," said William, stopping a passing waiter and corraling another drink. "*Carmen* is my favorite opera."

꙳

MARIO WAS EATING ALONE, soup and crackers—nothing else—still plagued by that hangover. "The drunkenest bunch of broads I ever seen," he grumbled to himself. "Not a one of them could have hit the ceiling with a baseball."

Reggie asked M-6 if he wanted more soup. M-6 merely grunted with disgust, and Reggie took the tureen away, thinking, "All the more for me."

The food that was wasted here was a scandal—except that it wasn't ultimately wasted. Reggie took it home with him. As a matter of fact, Reggie's kids were eating mighty fine, and Reggie was drinking fine.

A servant who had been recommended to M-6 by a caterer friend, Reggie, a black from Natchez, really knew his business. He'd worked in some mighty fine places, but there was nothing in his experience to equal this. For instance, in a millionaire's home in Lake Forest, the kitchen refrigerator had always been all but empty. The old guy was so tight he squeaked, as Reggie told his friends. Reggie went around hungry all day long. But not with Mr. Fanelli. This was the land of plenty—and not just plenty for Him, as in Lake Forest, but plenty for Reggie, too.

Mario rose from the table, lit a cigar, and with a groan lowered himself into a huge red and gold overstuffed chair that faced the big view window. Chicago lay spread out before him, with its crisscrossed boulevards and myriad lights, and at the far horizon to the west, there was a fire, the flames wavering up at times, then dying back. The faint thin whine of a police siren, like a locust call, rose to the penthouse. Mario sat staring down at Chicago with utter indifference.

ঙ

It was a little after nine in the morning, and Joe was patiently trying to work his way through a stack of reports when the phone rang.

"It's me," said a robust voice. "Dago Al. I'm sprung. When do we meet?"

Joe felt a rush of relief. So it was all right. He hadn't been taken for a sucker. "It'll have to be tonight," he said.

"All right," said Johnny Albert. "I got a good spot. No problem. Will you come?"

Joe said that he would, and Johnny gave him an address. It was on the near North Side, just off Sheridan Road, a rather good neighborhood—what Johnny had meant by a "good spot."

Joe arrived shortly after eight o'clock at a quite nice apartment-hotel, the Bristol Arms—and wondered vaguely to himself what the devil Giovanni was doing in a place like that.

A self-serve elevator took him to the fourth floor, where he found the right door with no trouble because loud music was going on inside and he could hear Johnny singing. Joe shook his head. Crazy. Always had been. Nothing bothered him.

Gina, all dressed up, let him in. She was a very good-looking girl at that, Joe noted—unusually so. Johnny came rushing to meet him and roughly dragged him into the middle of the living room. Johnny was big, strong, tough, and careless. He'd been the strongest boy in grammar school and had got into the most trouble—big Dago Al.

"Boy, have you changed!" cried Johnny, staring at Joe. "Man, have you changed! I'da hardly known you, Joe. You work hard for the cops—and for what?"

Johnny patted and hugged Joe and pummeled him around, and Joe finally extricated himself. Gina was staring at him with a puzzled expression.

"Let me tell you about this paisano," said Johnny.

"That's all you've been doing," said Gina as if resentful.

"Just listen, Mona Lisa . . ." said Johnny, then he turned to Joe. "That's what I call her, Mona Lisa— though she's better-looking. She's got this smile, see? And you don't know what it means—come and get it or drop dead."

"Drop dead is what it means," said Gina, and Johnny roared.

"Hey—how do you like this place?" he cried. "Gina was living here with some bum artist. A real one, I mean. He paints pictures. He even sells them. Look, here's one. Will you please for Christ's sake tell me what that picture means? It looks like two poached eggs on toast."

"You wouldn't know," said Gina. "You're too ignorant. That's an abstraction."

"So that's what it is. Well . . . up your abstraction with it. Eh, Joe . . . ?"

There was no way to cool him off. Joe decided on patience.

"Now I want to tell you about Joe," cried Johnny. "I was big, he was little—same age. I got all these other guys suckering up to me. Not Joe. So one day I took a poke at Joe. I thought he was a snotty brat. You know

44

what that sonofabitch did? He knocked me down. I was so surprised I didn't even kill him. Right, Joe?"

"Right," said Joe.

"Joe could have been a fighter. A guy was nuts to put the gloves on with Joe. So I wrassled him. I really bounced him around. One day he got so mad at me he kicked me in the balls."

"So that's what's the matter with you," said Gina.

Johnny roared. "Mona Lisa! Right? Oh, about this artist guy. I was on the lam kind of, you know. Trouble. So Gina moved in with this Everett guy. Met him in Gunter's Back Stage! You know—the restaurant in The Loop? Lonesome kind of guy, real nice. So then I'm back, and he says, 'Just take my apartment. I'm going to Paris and I won't be back for two months.' "

"They are giving him a one-man exhibition there," said Gina primly.

"Say, baby," said Johnny, "how about I give you a one-man exhibition?"

Gina threw Johnny a disgusted look, then said: "There is only one trouble here. Johnny will get us thrown out, he's such a goddamned loud-mouth."

Partially cooled, Johnny fell down into a chair and sat staring at Joe. "My old pal," said Johnny. "Long time no see."

"Yeah," said Joe.

"Well . . ." said Johnny, as if to say, now let's get down to work. Then he turned to Gina. "How about you rustle up something to eat—sandwiches, anything —okay?"

Gina looked from Johnny to Joe, then disappeared into the back.

"Good kid," said Johnny. "Remember old Brazzi, the tailor?"

"No," said Joe.

Johnny wagged his head in disgust. "I remember everything. You don't remember nothing. Brazzi's was right down the street from Sam's garage. Little guinea—couldn't speak English hardly; wore an earring, like the old people. Don't you remember old Brazzi? You lived around there."

Joe gestured, as if to say, so sue me.

"Well, Gina's his granddaughter. Hell, I'm old enough to be her father. She's nineteen . . . well . . . never mind Gina. I'll get around to her later." Johnny rose, went to a drawer and took out some maps, then put the maps on a table and sat across from Joe. "Now I'll give you the tale," he said. "I got in a little trouble on the North Side, with this dunce they had running the operation. He got on me pretty good—and hell, he's got these coked-up stoops on the payroll. If they come at me from the front, I could grind 'em up. But they sneak around and shoot you in the back. Well, I like to sleep at night. I knew this joker wasn't long for the world. He was a louse-up, see, and the boys don't like that. So I figured I'd hide till he got it. So I went way over in a neighborhood to the west, where they'd never look for me. Never find me except by accident. I was holed up nearly six months. And this was just recent, you understand.

"By the way," Johnny went on, "did you give Dave pictures of the missus?"

"Yes," said Joe.

"So I figured. All right. So I'm staying in mostly, except at night, when I'd make the local dives. Well, a guy can't sleep all the time, so I'd sit at the window, drink beer, smoke and stare out, like an old grandma with nothing better to do. Right? So I used to see this blonde. Sometimes she was walking, sometimes she was in a car with a guy. I thought, what a fine-looking broad. Then I had a shock. I thought to myself one day, good Christ, that looks like Joe Ricordi's wife. I seen her with you a couple of times—and you see her you don't forget . . ."

"Where did you see us?" asked Joe.

"Never mind. I seen you in places. The cops were looking for me at the time. And when you came in, I got out. Right, Joe, old pal? How'd I know you wouldn't put the arm on me?"

"So you think this was Maria . . . ?"

"Well . . . then I thought I was seeing things. Now I'm sure it was her. It burned my ass when I read it in the papers. Terrible. Some sonofabitch ought to have 'em cut off for that. But you know me—I'm no fink. Downtown'll tell you. But I got thinking after they grabbed me—maybe if I help Joe, he'll help me. And that's no routine fink, right?"

"Right," said Joe.

"No record of it . . . nothing. Right?"

"Right," said Joe.

"Well," Johnny went on, "I lived on a side street, cheap, you know—not too bad, but cheap; but only a block west was a wide boulevard with stores and hotels and apartment-hotels, real expensive places, and I always figured this woman lived in that area someplace; she was always going away from there or coming back to there. She seemed to like to walk. Sometimes I had the feeling she was just taking a walk, a stroll, you know. Sometimes I'd see her in a Cadillac with a guy . . ."

"Ever get a look at him?"

Johnny shook his head. "I never even tried. Joe, the

whole thing was . . . well, what do you say?—casual. It was only because I had nothing else to do I was looking down into the street at all. I seen lots of funny things, believe me. This woman was nothing to me. I didn't care who she was with . . ."

"You are sure it was Maria?"

"I am now. You see, Joe, at the time I didn't know you and the wife had busted up. If it wasn't Maria, it was a twin . . . I'll swear it was Maria."

"All right. Good," said Joe.

"Now," said Johnny, "here is a map of that section of town. I got it all marked off with crosses and darts and stuff. Where I stayed, the streets, which way she came, where she went, as far as I noticed. It ought to be a cinch. Dave just spreads his guys out through the shops and places, you know, with the pictures—and you may hit the jackpot. In fact I'll damn near guarantee it. Hell, she was the kind of woman people remember. Right? I only saw her a couple of times and fast, and I remembered. Right?"

"Right," said Joe. "Damn good job, Giovanni."

"Don't call me Giovanni," cried Johnny. "What do you think I am, a dago?" Johnny felt fine. He'd had his doubts. Would tough Joe feel he'd got enough for his five hundred clams? Joe was obviously pleased, with a lot of color coming into his gaunt face.

Joe took the maps and put them in his pocket.

"Thanks, Johnny," he said, and there was so much emotion in his voice that Johnny felt embarrassed and was glad that Gina took this moment to come in with a big tray of food. She'd even whipped up a little tray of antipasto to eat with their sandwiches, including olives and celery and radishes, and a huge pot of coffee.

"You know I can't eat radishes," said Johnny as

Gina spread the food around. "They make me belch."

Gina grimaced in disgust. "Johnny, you're such a crude . . ."

Johnny turned to Joe. "She's been like this ever since she lived with that pansy painter."

"He was no pansy," said Gina. "Far from it."

"All artists are pansies, or why would they do it?" cried Johnny.

"Because they have talent, that's why," said Gina disdainfully.

And while Johnny and Joe regaled themselves with Gina's neat and tasty meal—even the Italian sandwiches were not the usual unmanageable slabs—Gina rose, rummaged through a table drawer for a moment, and came back with a newspaper clipping she put down in front of Joe. Gina said nothing. She merely resumed her seat.

She had brought Joe an article from the Chicago *Tribune* dealing with the art of Ludlow Everett, native son, who had apparently done very well in Paris art circles, where he'd been exhibiting for ten years. Joe tried to read the article but he couldn't understand what it was saying. He noted the picture of Ludlow Everett, though: a long-faced man, in his forties, likely, with long hair and shell-rimmed glasses.

"You see?" said Gina. "He's even in the *Tribune*. They write articles about him. I've seen lots of others. He's got a scrapbook full of them. He made me a present of this one."

"Well . . ." said Johnny, "I kid a lot. But I thought he was an all-right guy. Lonesome, kinda. Just sat around and shot the breeze with us. Wouldn't you think he'd be sore when I popped up? Never turned a hair. Lemme tell you what he said about Gina. He said she was 'a delightful person.' " Johnny roared.

But Gina's pretty mouth tightened into a grim streak. "Well," she said, "that's better than you could do. Like, 'a riot in the hay, maybe, baby?' "

"Oh, don't get sore, Gina," said Johnny. "It's all in fun."

They ate in silence for a while, the two men relishing the food. Gina reached across the table for something, and Joe noted a small tattoo on her right forearm—it seemed to be letters, or something like that.

"What's that on your arm, Gina?" asked Joe.

Gina quickly withdrew her arm as if ashamed and looked at Johnny.

"I'm going to tell him," said Johnny, "since he asked. Okay, Gina?"

"Well . . ." said Gina dubiously.

"The tattoo says M-6," Johnny explained. "You ever hear of M-6, Joe?"

"No," said Joe.

"It's the big organization that runs all the whorehouses on the Southwest Side."

Joe couldn't help staring, surprised.

Gina seemed to wince. "Johnny, I don't know why you want to tell Joe about—"

"Because I'm proud of it, that's why." Johnny was one hood who hated the prostitution racket, and for a good and personal reason: He'd seen, as he said, too many fine Italian girls go that route. "Joe, I don't need to tell you all these houses have bouncers. Usually hoods down on their luck—they get lodging, food, and some dough. They keep the patrons straight, they keep the girls straight. Some of them are terrible bastards. Well, a hood named Jake borrowed money off me, didn't pay me back, and all of a sudden he disappeared. Finally I heard he was working over at a cat-house—" Gina winced again "—on the Southwest Side. So I went looking for him. He was working then; so he could pay me. But before I found him I got talking to Gina here—fine-looking Italian girl, right? And when she found out I knew her grandfather, old Brazzi, she gave me the tale. She was in hock and couldn't get out. They really stiff those girls. Charge them for clothes, all kinds of things—and take it out of what they got coming. Gina couldn't get away even if she wanted to—and she did. So . . . I stole her. Right, Gina?"

"Yes, right," said Gina, smiling at Joe, who seemed to be showing a sympathetic face for a change.

"Yeah, I stole her. And this stupid Jake comes following us, and I flattened him."

"My God," cried Gina, breaking in, "Johnny really did beat him around . . ."

"Well, he owed me money, and I hate welchers. But the hell with the money—I took it out in punches. Hell, I'm old enough to be Gina's father. She's only a kid, nineteen. Some kid, eh, Joe? Eh, Mona Lisa?"

Gina, smiling, reached over and patted Johnny on the back. "Sometimes I forget, Johnny."

"Just because I'm such a crude bastard and can't paint pictures that look like poached eggs, right?"

Gina stared at her plate.

"Yeah," said Johnny, "I stole her."

Joe was recovering from a mild case of shock. It was a terrible thing, girls getting mixed up in something like that, Italian or not; and for a moment Joe caught in his mind's eye a fleeting glimpse of his little blond, blue-eyed daughter, Maria—

Joe could hardly get away. Johnny wanted to talk

about the old days and all the guys they used to know and what had happened to them—much of it not very good, some of it appalling. Johnny remembered everything; Joe practically nothing. It was boring, and when he noted Gina yawning he made that his excuse to leave.

At the door he asked Gina: "You mean they made you put that tattoo on?"

"No," said Johnny, jumping in, "the kids just thought it was smart. Someday I'll bind and gag her and make her get it taken off . . ."

"It'll hurt like hell to get it taken off," said Gina. "A girl told me so."

"She probably had a sailing ship on her ass. This is nothing," cried Johnny.

"Well, it's my arm," said Gina, "so shut up."

Joe was just getting away when Johnny stopped him. "I didn't finish my story about the hideaway. See, I knew this creep, the guy I was having the trouble with, and thought he was something besides a straw boss—yeah, I knew it was only a question of time till he got it. Well, he got it. So I moved back."

Joe finally made the street.

◆§

JOE SAT on the edge of the bed in his pajamas, communing with himself. Or rather trying to talk some sense into his own head. All along he'd had a violent desire to do something, to strike—and here was his chance. If Johnny was right, it was a fairly simple matter to run down the place where Maria had lived, and there was a definite possibility—though Joe winced at the thought—that the man she'd been living with could be found.

From the start it had been tough for Joe to sit at his desk doing paperwork all day long—which is what an administrative job amounted to—while Dave Santorelli, in his patient plodding way, went about a case that was to him just another case, with maybe a little bit more urgency than usual because Maria had been a policeman's wife. Now, with a real hot lead, it would be even harder for Joe to sit still and wait, wait, wait.

And yet on the other hand what could he do—butt into Downtown's business? Assign himself illegally to a job already being covered? That Joe was a good police officer was recognized on all sides; he'd risen quickly. Would a good police officer even entertain such a preposterous idea? It just showed he wasn't thinking straight, hadn't been thinking straight for a long while. Time now to start thinking about the kids, not to mention his own future. . . .

Joe finally went to bed and tossed and turned. It was not always easy to do the right thing, even when you knew what it was, even in your own interests. Emotion was always a strong factor—very strong—but almost always a bad guide, as Joe had found out more than once. Like M-6, he decided to sleep on it.

≈§

It was a cloudy, lowering morning, the cloudiness making the heat worse but at least seeming to promise a clearing and cleansing rain. There was a thunderstorm in the air, with a kind of oppression in the atmosphere.

But Joe sat at his desk, oblivious to the weather, trying to restrain his impatience with the chief of detectives, Jim Mott, a grizzled veteran of the crime wars. Mott was complaining that his department was overworked and if some of the load wasn't taken off their backs, there would be trouble, like phony call-ins for illness and other maneuvers sometimes resorted to by the overworked force.

"Take it up with the lieutenant," said Joe, finally. "Why come to me?"

"Janowicz is off sick again, and there's no use trying to talk to the captain."

In short, Joe was in virtual command. The situation at Northwest was not good. The captain, Bernard "Tug" Farrell, was an old white-haired man always on the verge of retirement, a kind of monument in the city and the darling of the press because of his Irish wit, who was disgruntled because he'd never been appointed a deputy chief and now sat in his office all day and let the precinct run itself. Lieutenant Janow-icz was a sick man who wouldn't give in. Heart attacks were rumored, but he'd always denied them. Yet it was obvious that Janowicz was far from fit; he had an odd kind of pallor and a drawer full of pills of all colors that he seemed to take around the clock, or so it was said.

A few at the precinct didn't like Joe Ricordi, were put off by his manner, his unapproachability, which had grown over the years. But most did like him, and it was often said that Joe might turn out to be the youngest police captain in the city's history. Krum-packer, at the Southwest, was forty-five and he was spoken of as young. Joe's fortieth birthday was coming up toward the end of the year.

Joe listened to Mott's complaints till he got tired of them; then he said, "If everybody's so damned over-worked, how come I'm always stumbling over some of your guys at the water cooler?"

"Well, naturally I've got to have men around for emergencies . . ."

"And I've seen them playing cards," Joe went right on. "Can't they find anything better than that to do?"

"My men never play cards," cried Mott, outraged. "You must have seen some of those crazy reporters and—"

But Joe cut him off: "I'm going to recommend to the lieutenant that he get you all in and raise bloody hell with you. Nobody's getting worked to death. They all asked for the badge. Nobody twisted their arms. Maybe they ought to get into some other kind of work."

Mott glared at Joe for a moment, then got up and went out, passing Dave Santorelli in the hallway.

"Is Ricordi free now?" asked Dave.

"Free as the birds," said Mott with heavy sarcasm.

Dave turned to look after him, wondering.

Joe looked tough, unapproachable, even more so than usual, Dave thought. Apparently he'd just had more than a slight difference of opinion with old Mott. Dave settled himself into a chair in his slow, leisurely way and lit a cigarette. Joe just gestured, then got a map out of his drawer. He'd done the whole thing over himself, using Johnny's smudged and dog-eared and wrinkled original as his guide. It was all marked out neatly in red ink and as precise as if laid out by a draftsman.

Joe gave him the tale, not mentioning the source, of course. Then he carefully explained the map.

"Well, thanks for doing my work for me," said Dave.

"Every little bit helps."

"This, as you know, Joe, is not a little bit. This may

be it." Dave felt annoyed. He'd failed. Joe had succeeded. "I guess," said Dave, "your finks are better than mine."

Joe studied Dave's face for a moment, then he said, "It was a guy I used to know—years back. He came to me with it voluntarily. I haven't turned a hand on this case, Dave. It's yours."

Dave put the map away in his pocket, then leaned back in his chair and studied Joe. "Well," he said finally, "this may do it. The case is still open—suicide or murder. It may be murder one—that's the way we are proceeding. I'll get everybody they can spare on this right now. Okay, Joe?"

"Okay," said Joe.

Dave smoked for a while longer in silence, then got up and left, gesturing in reply to Joe's gesture. He still felt annoyed. But he was a fair-minded man, and little by little he admitted to himself that on this case he hadn't done well, not well at all. In fact, if the truth were known, he'd been slack, partly out of a feeling of hopelessness as he ran into one closed door after another, also partly because of the distracting problems he and his wife Frances were having with the teens. They'd rebelled against summer school, contending that they had more than enough school the rest of the year, so now it was a question of finding a couple of camps that weren't too expensive. And of course there was the baby, who did quite a lot of screaming at night. At times Dave was ashamed to find himself thinking: "There's got to be a better way than this."

Well . . . here was a prime lead. Would he bungle it? And just as he stepped outside the building, a sheet of lightning ripped the sky apart and it began to thunder as if there were a battle in progress beyond the horizon. Dave just barely made his car. The rain fell in appallingly heavy sheets, blotting out the world at times. This was hardly the day to start an exhaustive canvass of a neighborhood. And yet Dave decided that that was exactly what he intended to do, with five men —if Sluggo didn't scream too loud. The faster the better. To Sluggo, he'd predicate it on speed.

&

When the boys who hung around for Ted—Willie, Steve, Fatso, and Zell—said, "Meet you at Sadie's," you'd be lost if you didn't know that "Sadie's" was Zaida's, a large, well-fitted pool hall run by the Syrian, Zaida, who also pushed a little dope on the side—to the regulars, nobody else. Regulars could always get a fix—sometimes on the cuff, if they were regular enough; but a stranger couldn't get a pleasant look. But none of Ted's four used the stuff. Zell had kicked it and the other three had never touched it.

For them Sadie's was a hangout, a kind of headquarters where they played cards in the back, quarreled, lied, and sometimes drank too much, and where Ted could always find them from ten o'clock on. There was little or nothing for them to do during the day except in states of emergency.

The houses were open in the afternoon and there were quite a few customers of all varieties—businessmen treating themselves to a matinee, strangers from the hotels who had been "guided" by bellboys or taxi drivers, conventioneers who wanted a quick one as later they'd have no time for such things, what with meetings and parties—this crowd almost never caused any trouble. But after ten, sometimes earlier, the trouble started.

Ted could always be reached (no matter where he

went, he left the phone number), and Willie, Zell, Fatso, and Steve were on call. The houses even had stickups, and quite often fights, and tough drunks the resident bouncers couldn't handle. Backed by the others, Steve and Fatso generally brought order quickly by throwing bodies around. Fatso was big and fat and strong as an ox; Steve was just big and strong. But if they failed, Willie and Zell took over; they'd been known to gently carve up a real bad boy. If there was any shooting, it was done outside. Guys seldom brought guns into the houses. But it had been known to happen. A couple of years ago there had been quite a shoot-out in Maude's on the near North Side. Willie had got a bullet through his hat.

So Willie, Zell, Fatso, and Steve (and at one time Red Layton) were very useful to Ted and M-6, but their dangerous duties were never given a thought by themselves. When they weren't "working," they played cards or pool all evening long and gambled on anything anybody could name.

Tonight they were playing poker in a back room at Sadie's. Willie and Steve had been bickering all evening, both losing.

"Yeah," Steve was saying, "Willie's old man came over from sunny Italee with his grind organ, and Willie was the monkey."

"Well," said Willie, "they didn't get me out of no zoo—never had to keep me in a cage, like you. What was that the girl called you, the Missing Link? And maybe we come from Italy but we didn't come from no foreign country like Massachusetts, where they talk funny, like 'open de winder . . .'"

Everybody laughed, even Steve. He was a Massachusetts Irishman—Boston—and he did talk funny according to Chicago standards.

The bickering and the insults continued to fly as the cards flashed across the table and the money changed hands. Later the door opened and Sheffy came in apologetically, seeming to try to efface himself. Sheffy was a kind of pariah, a junkie who peddled secrets—anything he could find out. He was dangerous, and he lived dangerously and was very jumpy. He was such a mysterious creep that nobody had any idea what his real name was, or his nationality, or his place of origin. He was nondescript: thin, ordinary-looking, one of the millions.

"Hi, fellows," he said.

"You want something?" asked Willie.

"No, no. Just wanted to pass the time of day."

"If you got a bankroll you can sit in—no credit," said Steve.

Sheffy laughed self-consciously, putting his hand to his face like a kid. "Oh, no, you don't," he said. "You fellows are experts. I'm just a dub."

"Where have I heard that before?" Fatso put in.

"Well," said Sheffy, "I see everything's okay, you guys laughing it up."

"Why wouldn't it be?" asked Willie.

"Well, it mostly is, isn't it?" said Sheffy. "With that operation. Big stuff, right? Well, so long, fellows. Just thought I'd say hello. Gonna grab a lamb sandwich. Sadie just made some fresh."

At the mention of the lamb sandwiches, Steve and Fatso stampeded out, following Sheffy. But Willie and Zell remained.

Zaida sold food only as a convenience for the regulars, and you never knew what he would come up with: lamb pie, sometimes lamb or fish sandwiches, strange links of meat that were charred outside and rare inside, weird desserts that tasted like "sugared frost," as Steve said—little cakes, Syrian petit fours that tasted of pistachio, almonds, or cherries—and black coffee that you could float a spoon in.

This had all come about by accident. Zaida, a gourmet, loved to cook for himself. Occasionally he'd bring out a tidbit or so for a regular. They began to yell for more, and that was it.

Every day or so a Greek came in and pestered Zaida about jointly opening a restaurant. Zaida's fame had spread all over the neighborhood. But Zaida was doing too well as it was. Food was not his business; he just enjoyed dabbling in it.

"What do you mean he was getting at something?" said Zell.

"He was. He was," said Willie.

"Hell, we didn't tell him nothing, Willie," said Zell.

Zell decided he'd go out and get some coffee. Nothing was served at Zaida's. Every man was his own waiter. But Willie sat on. He had a hunch something was up. But what? Sheffy in and out like that; it didn't make sense.

◆§

TED WAS FEELING RESTLESS, at loose ends. Helga had been trouble, constant trouble, no doubt about it, but she had also been a companion, something Ted had really not had before. Prior to the time of Helga, Ted's sexual relations had consisted of a steady parade of strangers through his elegant fifth-floor apartment; it got so for a while he could hardly tell one from another. Helga had changed all that, and since her death he had never really resumed his former mode of life. He'd had a girl here and there, but they left him feeling not only restless but bored.

Lately he'd had his eye on the brunette, Melanie, at Wally's Piano Bar, but Melanie had a mind of her own and a life of her own and was no easy mark; far from it. It would take time, and time was something Ted did not have a lot of, especially now that things were touch-and-go because of Helga.

All right, the uproar had died down and Bones had seemed satisfied. But you could never be easy with Bones, and things might change in a day, in an hour.

Ted finally decided he'd go out to the piano bar and have a little talk with Melanie, and he was just reaching for the phone to call Willie at Zaida's to tell him where he'd be when it rang. Ted answered it. The voice on the other end seemed muffled. The sound of it worried Ted, and he immediately began to get nervous.

"My name is Sheffy," said the voice. "Do you know who I am?"

"No," said Ted. "How did you get this number?"

"Never mind that. I've got info for you."

"Well, what is it?"

"It will cost you five C's. Meet me at the book rack at Wiggins's in fifteen minutes. If you are not there by that time, I'll leave—no dice. I can sell this someplace else . . ."

Ted noted that his hand was shaking. "What's it about? Give me some idea."

"It's about maybe you'd like to live a little longer." The connection was abruptly broken.

Ted just stood there with the phone in his hand. What should he do? Why not let Willie handle it? His own way. Willie could pay the fink or get rid of him, whichever Willie thought best. Or why not just ignore it altogether? But that, Ted decided, he simply could not do, especially at a time like this. Said Sheffy was no doubt one of that unlovely breed, an information peddler. Maybe he really had something. Curiosity began to get the best of Ted.

He counted the money in his wallet, slipped out five one-hundred-dollar bills, and put them in a side pocket. Then he clipped a police-type holster to his belt and put his .38 in it. A stranger would never think that the elegantly attired Ted Beck, with the curly blond locks and the air of a prosperous salesman, would be handy with a gun, but he was; very handy. Now he had men to worry about work of that kind, but in the past he'd had to do his own.

Wiggins's was a very large drugstore on the boulevard corner near Ted's apartment-hotel where they sold everything, it was said, but drugs. And it was usually crowded till midnight. Tonight was no exception. Sheffy had picked a perfect spot for his own safety.

Ted entered and looked about quickly, then moved down through the crowd to the place he'd noticed at the far end where there were turnable racks filled with paperbacks of all descriptions, mostly of the nudie-girly type. He noticed a little man in a black, pin-striped suit and a collar that was too big for his neck glancing his way over the paperback in his hand, and Ted moved over to him.

"I'm Sheffy," said the man, talking prison-style, without moving his lips. "Got the money?"

Ted nodded, saying nothing.

"Well, let me have it," said Sheffy.

"I'll judge if the info's worth it," said Ted.

"It may be worth a million. Now give me the money or forget it."

Ted hesitated. Apparently this guy knew his business. But if it was a mere con, Ted could collar him easily in this crowd. He gave Sheffy the money. Sheffy examined it briefly, put it in his pocket, then turned his back on Ted and appeared to be studying a paperback.

"Mr. Beck," he said, "five coppers are fanning out in this neighborhood with very fine pictures of a certain lady. They can't miss, as they are working their way west, and tomorrow they'll be right on this corner."

"Thanks," said Ted, then hurried out.

ぅ

IT WAS VERY CROWDED and noisy in the main room at Zaida's, with all the pool tables in use and many kibitzers sitting along the walls in high chairs. And in the back room Willie, Fatso, Steve, and Zell were still playing cards and drinking what Zaida insisted was Syrian wine, though it tasted more like medicinal tonic. Willie didn't seem to have much interest in the game and kept glancing at his wristwatch.

"Come on, Willie, deal," yelled Steve, a little high on the Syrian wine. "What the hell's the matter with you tonight? You're losing and you don't care."

"It's after midnight," said Willie. "I was figuring we'd hear from the boss."

"To hell with the boss," yelled Steve. "So it's quiet. What's the matter—you looking for work, trouble? Deal the cards."

Willie passed the deal, to his companions' disgust, then got up and started out.

"Come on, come on," yelled Steve, turning. "Three-handed's no good."

But Willie ignored them and went out. Steve picked up the deck and slammed it down hard on the table, and cards flew in every direction.

Fatso laughed and sat back comfortably. "Well, this is fine with me. I'm over three C's ahead."

But Zell said, "Willie's been worried all evening. Something about that creep Sheffy. I don't know what."

Willie came back in hurriedly. "I'm going over to Ted's. I can't get him on the phone, and either he didn't leave a number to call or there's a screw-up at the apartment."

"He didn't leave a number to call?" Steve seemed stunned.

"I said it might be a screw-up," said Willie angrily. "Now you guys stay put."

❧

WILLIE ENTERED THE big apartment-hotel by way of the garage. After all, Willie was spoken of as Mr. Beck's chauffeur around the place. The first thing he noted was Ted's Cadillac in its stall. He took the elevator to the lobby and talked to the night man, who knew nothing. Hadn't seen Mr. Beck or heard from him.

"There's something wrong here," said Willie. "Give me the key; I'll check upstairs. And you look through the stuff. Maybe he left a number for me to call and the other guy mislaid it."

"That could be," said the nightman patiently.

"Anybody else around?"

"Yes," said the nightman. "A bookkeeper's working in the office and the night engineer's here."

"Ask around," said Willie, then he took the key and left.

Willie let himself in very quietly. He was going to look damned silly if Ted had taken a few too many and was just sleeping it off, not hearing the phone. Not that Ted was a drunk, but now and then, especially when he was out with a broad, he belted the juice pretty good. Willie stood in the little foyer listening. Not a sound. He tiptoed to the bedroom door and listened, then he slowly opened it and peered in. Light from the living room showed the big bed to be empty, unslept in. Then Willie began to look about him with growing apprehension. Oh, what a stink if Ted had lammed. And if he'd lammed, why?

Willie switched on the lights in the bedroom and examined it. Plenty of clothes—but Ted had an excess and maybe he'd just gathered up a few for a quick sprint. Willie returned to the living room and, remembering the small wall safe he'd seen Ted open many times, crossed to it. The safe door was ajar and the safe was empty. That did it. Willie began to swear to himself and stamp around.

Naturally Ted wouldn't take the car. It would be a dead giveaway, its license a matter of record. Suddenly it came to Willie in a flash—Sheffy; he'd known there was something fishy. Sheffy had cased Zaida's to see if they were all in the back room, safe and sound. Then he went out and braced Ted and gave him some Sheffy info. What?

Willie went to the phone and got Zell at Zaida's and gave him the following instructions: "You three guys comb every joint you can think of. Fan out. Find Sheffy. Tell him I want to talk to him—no beef, nothing. I just want to talk to him, understand? But if he won't come, drag him. Okay?"

"Okay," said Zell.

In the lobby the nightman motioned for Willie to come to the desk.

"Got something?"

"Yes," said the nightman. "The bookkeeper went out for coffee and he saw Mr. Beck get in a taxi out front."

"Well, then I guess everything's all right," said Willie, smiling. "Thanks for your trouble."

⋅≼ჟ

ZELL, STEVE, AND FATSO brought Sheffy in the back way at Zaida's shortly after three A.M. They had to carry him, he was so scared. He considered himself to be a dead man. But Willie quickly got a couple of drinks into him and sat him on a chair. A little color began to come back into Sheffy's face when it became apparent that Willie did not intend to kill him—at least not yet.

"All right," said Willie, "why didn't you come to us with the info?"

"Because I knew Mr. Beck would pay more," said Sheffy, on the verge of tears.

"All right. What's the info?"

Sheffy gave it to them at great length, nervous, almost hysterical, repeating himself, even contradicting himself, and he was appalled to note that these four brutes kept drawing back and looking at each other as he told the tale.

"Sheffy," said Willie, "I'm going to let you get away with this. Why should I bother with your worthless hide? But from now on, you come to me. Understand? Come to me."

Steve slammed Sheffy across the face and Sheffy

seemed to sail through the air before he hit the floor.

"That's so you'll remember," said Steve.

᪥

Bones hadn't been sleeping well lately, so he was more than half-awake when the phone on his nightstand rang.

It was Willie with his disastrous tale. Shocked, Bones said nothing for a moment, thinking: "Mario was right and I was wrong." Then he got himself together and said to Willie, "We've got to move Kemper up as of right now. I'll see to it. And you get on Ted, Willie. He's got to be found. And I'll see what I can do with Krumpacker."

"Right," said Willie.

Bones hung up the phone, then just sat for a moment, staring. Finally he fumbled around nervously, found his cigarettes, and lit up. Gray was beginning to show at his windows. Soon a new day would be dawning. Maybe a catastrophic day for all of them.

᪥

But at least they did their best to fend off disaster by efficiency. Before Dave Santorelli and his men were once more on the street, Kemper had been installed as the new boss of the houses; Willie, Fatso, Zell, and Steve had disappeared from the Zaida area without a trace; and Bones had briefed Mario Fanelli, who didn't even say, "See, I told you so." He merely groaned.

Now Mario had a big problem of his own—The Man. As usual, it was M-6 who had to take the responsibility and the heat; that's what he was getting paid for.

As for Kemper, he was a kind of accident and a temporary expedient at best. He was a CPA who had been keeping the houses' books (for M-6) for some time now. Gradually he'd given up his former work, moved into the Southwest Side, and become one of them, as he often said, trying to make it sound funny. He was a loner now whose wife had divorced him and taken the kids, one reason being that Kemper, after many years of what he considered to be deprivation, had taken to the whores. In short, he was a conventional guy, a straight john, who had gone through a slow process of corruption.

His ability to handle the houses as boss was doubtful, and his ability to manage the likes of Willie, Fatso, Steve, and Zell was more than doubtful. Steve called him Eyeshade because he had the habit of wearing one whenever he was working with figures, which was constantly. But now he would be not Eyeshade but Mr. Kemper . . . at least for a while.

Kemper had seemed nervous all through his long interview with Willie, saying little, and he seemed more nervous when confronted with Fatso, Steve, and Zell.

"We figure," said Willie, "you'll want to keep us on. But . . . if you've got your own guys, just say so."

"No, no," said Kemper. "You men are just fine with me."

So Willie and his men relocated themselves, and little by little things began to get straightened around, though it was no cinch to install a new regime, which is one reason so many mediocre bosses are put up with and manage to hang in there.

At one time Ted Beck was considered to be the best man M-6 had. But Ted had not worked out as well as expected, and had finally pulled what The Man always called a dummy. Dummies could be very costly, both to those who pulled them and to those they worked for. Ted had pulled one of the most colossal, and the end of its ramifications was not yet in sight; far from it.

᪣

Bones was having lunch at Chancy's and had just reached dessert when Dom, one of the table captains, brought him a phone and plugged it in for him. Dom was a pleasant fellow, and Bones had always been inclined in his favor until one day Dom had disclosed that Sergeant Joe Ricordi of the Northwest Precinct was his brother; since then Bones had been coldly polite and uncommunicative. Dom had figured that as a lawyer who was around courts, Mr. Macready might know Joe. Dom seemed very proud of his brother, but Bones took a dim view of the police. He was inclined to judge them all by the police he and M-6 dealt with, though actually he knew better.

Over the phone Bones received the following message: "You will please go to your apartment and stand by."

So Bones went to his apartment and stood by. This meant The Man was going to call. Sometimes he didn't call for hours, but you stood by all the same. You'd better stand by. He seldom called. When he did, he expected it to be considered an event in your life.

This time he called almost as soon as Bones got home. Although Bones tried hard not to admit it, even to himself, The Man's infrequent calls shook him up badly, made him apprehensive and nervous. What was The Man, after all, but a stepped-up version of Mario? Easy to say!

"Mac?" came The Man's thick voice. He always talked as if he had a head cold or should have his tonsils out, and he was the only man in Chicago who called Bones Mac. "A pretty fine mess we've got, yes?"

The Man still had a touch of Brooklyn accent, though he'd lost most of it.

"I've seen worse," said Bones.

"What do you think? Can Mario handle it?"

This jolted Bones slightly. "I think so."

"Don't lie to me, Mac," said The Man. "Level. You're a smart guy. That's why I pay you all that money. I don't like these dummies, these louse-ups. No good. I like it smooth. You know that. Now level."

"It can never be perfect."

"You're telling me? Perfect—for Christ's sake. It's always something with these bums I'm cutting in for big. Can't nobody do nothing right? Where does Mario get these bums he has working for him, out of some insane asylum? Can't even weight a broad. Christ, a ten-year-old kid could do that."

There was a pause. Bones waited.

"Listen, Mac," The Man went on, "I want you to keep an eye on Mario. All he does is lay broads and drink. Level with me. If he can't do the job, I want him out. Jesus, I got a hundred things to worry about."

"I don't say he's perfect," said Bones, "but he knows the business and he'll give you a straight answer, yes or no."

"He says he wanted to get rid of Ted and you advised against it. Right?"

Bones hesitated, feeling a slight chill. "Well, we talked it over and he decided to give Ted another chance."

"Well, that's no matter anyway," said The Man. "Now, Mac, I'm counting on you. If you think Mario can't handle it, I want you to say so. Understand?"

"I understand."

Pause; then The Man said: "Say, I won a big bet for a change, Mac. A beautiful fix and this Kentucky guy cut me in on it. Ten thousand bucks on the nose at three to one. I'm still celebrating. 'Bye, Mac."

So The Man was gambling again! Bones had heard that in one year The Man had lost over a million dollars at the tracks, horse and dog. And that was a joke to make a horse laugh: The Man as a sucker gambler.

Bones poured himself a stiff drink, sat down, relaxed, and tried not to admit to himself what his true position was—a kind of super Willie. Willie watched the whorehouse boss—and good old William Macready watched the guy who bossed the guy who ran the houses.

Bones tried to laugh it off. "Who says crime doesn't pay?" But today his own humorous thoughts did not strike him as funny. He felt jittery. But then he always felt jittery after talking with The Man. Maybe he'd call up Daphne this evening and they'd go out for a night on the town. It's true Daphne was a kind of pleasant bore, but he was always proud to be seen with her, the height of fashion, even if she was a little long in the tooth—his own age at least, maybe older. And if he got tired of the rat race finally, he might even marry Daphne and help her spend her money.

The death of a rich father and a rich husband had

insured Daphne's future. She no doubt had money she didn't even know about, and it was well managed by the executors, the Farmers and Drovers Bank of Chicago. Quite a few guys had their eyes on that money, but Daphne was no fool; far from it. She was a smart lady, almost immune to the con.

Bones poured himself another drink and sat thinking. He just didn't feel very happy today.

◦§

DAVE SANTORELLI'S MEN were getting close. From negative, the results were now turning positive. Helga had been recognized by at least half a dozen people, who said they'd often seen her in the neighborhood but didn't know who she was or where she lived. But finally Detective Otto Weiner hit pay dirt. A man in an electrical-appliance store across from Wiggins's drugstore said: "Sure I know who that is. I don't mean I really know who it is. But it's a lady who lives right down the street, at the Excelsior."

Weiner called the station, the station called Dave, and half an hour later they both appeared in the lobby of the Excelsior apartment-hotel, showed their badges to a bewildered day man, then the picture of Helga.

"Of course I know who it is," said the day man nervously. "It's Mrs. Beck, but she's not here anymore."

"Where did she go?" asked Dave, straight-faced.

"I don't know," said the day man. "On a trip, I suppose. Her husband's here, though."

Dave and Otto exchanged a look. But it turned out that her husband was not there. So while Otto remained on stakeout in the lobby, Dave checked with

Downtown about Ted Beck. Was anything known about him? The people at the Excelsior seemed to know nothing at all. He seemed to have no friends, at least none that the hotel personnel knew anything about. There was only Willie, the chauffeur. But the Excelsior had no address for Willie.

⁓§

Dave debated with himself for a long time on just how to handle this matter as far as Sergeant Joe Ricordi was concerned. As Sluggo had said, it was delicate. How and why would Mrs. Ricordi get mixed up with a hood? Dave winced when he thought of the interview, but feeling it was his duty, he decided it would be better to talk with Joe in the privacy of his home than at his office in the Northwest Precinct. Joe could wrestle with the problem much better alone than surrounded by fellow officers. Tomorrow it would hit the papers. Not hard, of course, but an item would appear. "Suspect sought in the case of. . . ." With sketchy but pertinent details.

Dave found Joe washing the dishes. Tonight Joe had decided to whip himself up some dinner, but he'd stalled around, taking a shower, listening to the radio, goofing off so long rather aimlessly, feeling at loose ends, that it was after eight o'clock before he had sat down to the table. Dave, used to lending a helping hand around the house, picked up a dish towel and went to work.

"Well," said Dave, responding slowly to looks from Joe, "your map did it, Joe. We've got a suspect."

Joe paused in the middle of a dish. "Yeah? Who?"

"His name is Taddeus Byscznski. Alias Ted Beck."

"Well . . . what about him?"

Dave hesitated, then plunged on. "Apparently Mrs. Ricordi was . . . well, they were living together as man and wife."

Joe stopped as if shot; he seemed to go rigid. Then without comment he resumed his work.

"He's a bad one, Joe. A hood, with a typical hood record. Assault. Aggravated assault. He just missed manslaughter. A pusher he beat up was given up for dead once, but finally survived. But for five years he's been clean, nothing on his record. He'd obviously hit it big some way. This apartment-hotel's an expensive place."

"Well . . . is he in custody?"

"No," said Dave. "Can't be found. Somebody must have warned him. He left the night before."

Long pause, then as they finished up their task at the sink, Joe said: "With that kind of guy . . . looks like murder, doesn't it?"

"Yes," said Dave, "it does. And I've got every guy I can pry loose from the lieutenant on it. We'll find him, Joe. Wiley's combing the finks. And Sergeant Murtaugh's got two special men in the field working on it. They know every hood in the metropolitan area."

Joe got out the Chianti bottle and poured them a drink and they sat for a long time in silence. Dave was very uncomfortable. He'd noted that once more the color had drained out of Joe's face.

"Joe," said Dave, finally, "can I make a suggestion?"

"Why not?"

"The guy who gave you the info—the map? Maybe he might know something. I figure he's an insider."

"But he's no fink, Dave. He's done his part."

Another long silence, then Dave finished off his

drink and rose. They looked at each other for a moment, then Dave held out his hand and they shook. Dave felt even more uncomfortable than when he'd arrived. Joe needed help. But Dave didn't know what kind. Besides, he was immersed in troubles of his own. Dave had the crazy feeling he was deserting Joe as he gestured and left.

Joe sat on, oblivious to his surroundings, not noting how cool it had turned or the noisiness with all the windows open or that all the lights in the flat were on. He felt stunned. Maria and a hood? He'd envisioned anything but that. For three years he'd tried not to picture anybody . . . he had fought hard against facing the obvious. Now here it was, right before his eyes— and he was still unwilling to face it. Could there be some kind of mistake? A misidentification in regard to Maria? Johnny hadn't been exactly sure . . . only pretty sure. . . .

Joe's thoughts went around in circles as the clock ticked on, a cool lake breeze blew, and the street outside was unusually noisy with traffic . . . and nothing seemed to make any sense at all in a crazy world.

৽

AT THE SOUTHWEST PRECINCT Captain Krumpacker was not his usual smiling self. He'd had a long telephone conversation with Bones and he was burning with anger. (In the outer hallway Cyrus D. Travis III was waiting patiently to take the captain to a luncheon. It was a special occasion and Alderman Hruba had condescended to put in an appearance.) With the captain were two special deputies, troubleshooters: Fiore and Maxon.

"It's your job to find him," the captain was saying.

"Never mind Downtown or Murtaugh or anybody. He operated within our jurisdiction, right? Find him —and I'll remind you he is a hoodlum, armed and dangerous. Do I make myself clear?"

"Right, Captain," said Fiore, and Maxon nodded.

A few minutes later Fiore and Maxon passed Cyrus D. in the hallway and gestured a greeting. Cy wondered if Alderman Hruba's words had struck home. Very likely. But he didn't know about the most important pressure laid on: Bones's.

Nearly a quarter of an hour passed, but finally Captain Krumpacker emerged from his office, looking slim and fit and spic and span as usual, though his smile seemed a little forced.

"Shall we take my car or an official car?" asked Cy, rising.

"Since it's a special occasion," said the captain, "we'll take an official car."

"After you, Captain," said Cy, stepping aside and gesturing the way to the elevator.

◆§

TED COULDN'T MAKE UP his mind what to do. It was easy to say lam. But where? Even with money it was no simple proposition. He'd bought a car for cash on the South Side and then driven clear across town at night, to the far North Side, where he'd stayed in a motel for one night only. He felt uncomfortable on the far North Side; it was alien territory to him. As for fleeing the city, Ted winced from that. He knew nobody anyplace and had never been out of Chicago in his life, except for once or twice to Gary, Indiana. And what the hell could he do in Gary?

And so Ted wound up back on the Southwest Side in a neighborhood alien to him but not too far from familiar places and things. He could trust nobody; nobody. Not only were the police after him, M-6 was also. He was in a real life-or-death bind. But he'd been in one before and had come out of it, and he'd been only twenty-one at the time, a scared punk.

He'd found a one-bedroom apartment in a good spot. Just beyond his windows was a low hill with a steep incline, a poor approach for a killer. The apartment was in a five-dwelling complex, a renovated job with confusing exits and entrances, a kind of warren. It was not an easy place for a stranger to find his way around in, and two of the families living there were Poles who hardly spoke English at all and kept severely to themselves. It was strictly a lower-class, straight-john neighborhood, very quiet at night. There wasn't a speak, a club, or a pool room within miles. It was a worker's place. And Ted felt reasonably safe.

The question was how long could he hold out living an unnatural, hermitlike life like this? And what was he holding out for? One thing: the heat to be off. When would that be and how? Ted always examined those questions gingerly. A guy had to have some kind of hope.

&§

THE HOT WEATHER had returned. Joe sat in his shirt-sleeves, eating a bowl of minestrone and drinking iced tea. All the windows were open, and there was not a breath of air as the city sweltered. It was Fourth of July weather. This was the third and already firecrackers were snapping in the neighborhood, and from time to time skyrockets went up from in among the rooftops.

Today had been a bad one, including a run-in with the lieutenant over Chief of Detectives Mott, who had put on quite a whine to the lieutenant about what Joe had said to him. "Goddamn it, Joe," the lieutenant kept yelling, "you know these men are overworked." But Joe held his ground, and Janowicz finally had such a coughing and choking spell that he nearly scared Joe to death. Janowicz turned white as chalk, then red as he kept choking, trying to get his breath. Joe called the infirmary and a medic finally appeared, then a doc. But at last Janowicz got himself together, though he seemed shaky. Joe told the lieutenant he was sorry for stirring him up so, but Janowicz just waved him out. Later somebody drove Janowicz home.

Janowicz should give it up, Joe thought. But he just wouldn't, and the captain never seemed to notice the problem, or care, if he did.

Joe finished his soup and his tea, then turned the radio on and tried to read a paper. Once he'd been very much interested in the sports section, but now he'd sort of lost track. When he was in high school, he used to know the batting averages of all the players in the major leagues; now he didn't even know the players.

There was a tap at the door. Santorelli? But it was a rather apologetic-looking Johnny and a seemingly embarrassed Gina. Johnny was carrying a package wrapped in a newspaper.

"Can we come in?" asked Johnny.

Joe gestured them in but decided that if Johnny started to make a habit of this, he'd just have to level with him. A hood like Johnny was not exactly an ideal companion for a sergeant of the Chicago police department.

"Look what I brought you," cried Johnny, displaying a tall, slim bottle of yellow liquid. "Liquore Galliano, Joe. The real thing. From Milano. See the label? Green, white, and red. My new boss has got a whole closet full of it, so I clouted this. What does he need with all them bottles, right, Joe?"

Joe couldn't help laughing. Once a teacher had said that Giovanni would steal a fire plug if he could get it loose from the cement. He got out some small glasses, and Johnny opened the bottle and poured.

Joe had never tasted Galliano before. It was delicious.

Johnny held his glass up to the light, sipped it, and said: "I wonder what the poor people are doing tonight."

Gina seemed very quiet. She moved away from them, sat in Joe's chair, and listened to the radio, or pretended to. Johnny noted that Joe was observing Gina and said: "Don't mind her. She's nervous tonight. Maybe it's because she gets this letter from the artist. Right, Gina?"

"I'm not nervous," said Gina. "You guys like to talk, and you never talk about anything that interests me."

"Well, we ain't artists, right? The only kinda pictures we like are dirty postcards. You should read this letter from the guy . . ."

"He just took my letter and read it," said Gina resentfully. "He's such a bum."

"He said he had lunch up on the Eiffel Tower and he got to thinking about Gina. What a con artist! How can you have lunch up on top of that tower? That's stupid. He said he saw a picture in some kind of museum . . ."

"The Louvre," Gina put in. "It was by Boucher."

"Will you listen to this broad!" cried Johnny. "Anyway, the con artist said the picture reminded him of Gina, and he was going to copy it and give it to her when he got back, or maybe send it to her . . ."

"I wish to God he'd asked me to go with him," cried Gina.

"He's got her spoiled rotten," said Johnny. "Drink your Galliano. That's choice stuff. But she never thanks me for anything."

Gina remained silent, and Joe vaguely wondered about her. Had Everett changed her life as drastically as Maria had changed his? It was very likely.

Johnny tried to keep talking it up, but finally he too fell silent and Joe began to realize that this was not just a social visit. They had something on their minds but apparently didn't know how to spring it. Johnny refilled the glasses all around, then sank down into a chair beside Gina and listened to the radio. Joe sat at the table slowly relishing the Italian liqueur.

Finally Johnny broke the ice. "Joe, we've got something to say . . ."

"Why not?" said Joe.

"Christ, pretty soon a copper like you will tag me for a fink. But it's just because we want to help you, Joe. You helped us. Right, Gina?"

"Yes," said Gina, "when that Melvin would hardly give me the time of day."

"That bastard," said Johnny. "I'm surprised somebody hasn't cooled him long ago."

Silence again; but Joe refused to help them. If they had something to say, let them say it. He wasn't going to drag it out of them.

Finally Johnny jumped up and began to pace. Then he spoke abruptly. "Joe—have they identified the guy?"

"What guy?"

Johnny squirmed. "That Beck guy, like it said in the papers."

"What do you mean, have they identified him? Of course they have. Where do you think they got the name? They've got his record."

Johnny exchanged a long look with Gina. "Do they know who he is? What his job was?"

"No," said Joe.

"M-6," said Johnny. "He ran all the whorehouses."

Gina grimaced in embarrassment and irritation. Joe said nothing, but Johnny noticed he seemed to turn pale, or maybe it was the light.

At that moment there was yelling and carrying on in the street below, and they hurried to the window and looked down. Apparently a defective skyrocket had refused to rise or had fallen prematurely. It was now skittering all over the street and people were running in every direction. The skyrocket finally sputtered into darkness, and they turned away from the window.

"Are you sure about this, Johnny?" Joe demanded after a long silence.

"Ask her. This is her ball game."

"Has to be," said Gina. "And I read it in the paper and then I told Johnny. The girls were always talking about Ted Beck. I never saw him. But he was the boss."

Joe fell silent again. The Galliano no longer pleased his palate. How could things just keep getting worse?

Long silence. Johnny and Gina grew very uncomfortable.

"Well," said Johnny, rising, "Gina told me about it, and we just thought it might help."

"Yes," said Joe, with an effort. "It should help."

A short time later Johnny and Gina left, silent, rather embarrassed. Joe's attitude shook and puzzled them. He couldn't seem to bring out a word without almost painful effort.

Once in the street, Johnny said: "I think he figures that . . . well, maybe this Beck bastard promoted Maria for the trade. Joe's a good Catholic, you know. It's gotta hit him hard. He's not like me; I never gave a damn about nothing. Joe always did."

✿

JOE FELT not only stunned, but bewildered. It was hard to believe. In fact, Joe almost persuaded himself not to believe it. For a long time he paced the room, enraged one moment and pushing the whole sordid story away from himself the next. Could this all be the result of a misidentification by Johnny of Maria? Were they barking up the wrong tree, following a phantom trail. . .?

Little by little Joe calmed down and made up his mind what to do. No matter how repugnant and enraging the idea was to him, no matter how hard he had to struggle against his desire merely to deny and evade, the matter simply must be followed up. He called Dave Santorelli at his home and rather haltingly explained.

A blank silence was the reply, but finally Dave said (after a quiet whistle of amazement): "It's a cinch this guy is a very popular man right now, with not only us looking for him. Well, Joe, this ought to help a lot, and I wish I had a line of communication like yours."

"It was volunteered," said Joe bluntly, not liking the implications.

"All right. I'll take it up with the lieutenant first thing in the morning. Wait till Murtaugh gets the word. What a roust there is going to be around town. Oh, man!" Dave seemed awed. He tried to think of something more to say, something soothing, as Joe was no doubt taking this hard. But what could you say to Joe Ricordi? Dave couldn't think of anything. He merely said good-bye and hung up.

Joe poured himself a glass of wine and sat looking blankly out the window, seeing nothing. He was still in a state of shock and bewilderment. How could such things be?

ᴇᔍ

BONES WAS ATTENDING a large dinner party in the banquet room of a Gold Coast hotel. The party was being given by Mr. and Mrs. Ben Mosely, of the Mosely Iron Works, and Daphne was co-hostess, and Bones, or rather William, was her guest. The waiters were in colonial costumes and there were little American flags topping the rum cake. A kind of champagne flowed freely.

A string trio provided the music, and with the coffee a redheaded, bob-haired young baggage appeared in an Uncle Sam costume (except for the skintight satin shorts) singing and dancing "I'm a Yankee Doodle Dandy" to vociferous applause, and she stirred things up so much that many rose from the table and marched around the room singing with her. She was called back for four encores.

"She makes me nervous," said William.

"Why is that?" asked Daphne, above the uproar.

"I'm afraid she'll split those pants."

Daphne put on an outraged face but couldn't restrain her laughter. "Oh, William," she said. "How can you say such things?"

It turned out to be quite a party. William sat back comfortably enjoying his cigar and for once allowed himself to be lazy and thoughtless and don't-give-a-damn, an unusual attitude of mind for him, who normally had moves, plans, strategems, and even fears crowding into his mind around the clock.

But his euphoria didn't last very long. He was called away. Very important. But he took his time about making his apologies and he told Daphne that he hoped to get back shortly, but if he did not, he would check with her at home.

"Oh, this is too bad," cried Daphne. "Business simply can't be this important. It's why so many of you die young."

William felt like thanking her for the kind words. Young he'd never be again. Next month—fifty. Half a century. Appalling!

◦§

BONES AND M-6 were a very incongruous pair tonight: Bones in his dinner coat, starched shirt, and black butterfly tie, and M-6 in a yellow silk undershirt, white duck pants, and red socks—and sweating as usual. It was the night of the Fourth of July, and from their vantage point high above the city, they could see rockets going up all over the whole area.

Tonight Mario was not his usual slack, indifferent-seeming self. He looked tough and formidable.

"Goddamn, what a louse-up, and The Man climbing all over me," he said. "So here is what I'm going to do. I'm going to handle this Ted business myself. I got two bird dogs who could find a guy if he were dead and buried, and they are going to find this bastard, blast him, and dump him. . . ."

"Wait a minute," said Bones.

"You keep still. Let me talk. I been listening to you too much. Just sit there."

Bones felt a flash of anger but composed himself.

"You know what I'm talking about?" cried Mario. "All these silly bastards running around and nothing happening. Willie and the other guys—and they couldn't find an elephant in a supermarket. So I'm supposed to sit back and wait? To hell with that. I'm putting these guys on—for big money—and you call them clowns off, as I don't want them getting in the way."

"Did you talk to The Man about this?"

"I'm handling this, I'm handling this," yelled Mario. "You know the last thing he said to me? He said, 'Now you handle it, you dirty dago bastard.' That's what The Man said. What does he think *he* is, a Polack?"

Bones didn't like this kind of talk. Mario was getting out of hand. He'd been belting the juice and obviously he just wasn't thinking straight.

"Mario," said Bones, "listen to me. This is not a good idea. Willie is—"

"Don't tell me about Willie. Don't try to alibi for them bums. I'm just not going to sit here and wait. You understand? And don't give me anymore of your gentlemanly 'I wouldn't do that' routine—I'm getting

goddamned sick and tired of it, and of you, Mr. Macready. You are a con artist, conning money out of us
suckers who listen to you. And that's what I told The
Man . . ."

Bones got to his feet, feeling a kind of brutal cold
anger. "And what did he say?"

"And what did he say?" Mario was mimicking
Bones, trying to parody his precise manner of speak-
ing. "I told you what he said. He said, 'Now you
handle it, you dirty—' "

"I heard it the first time," said Bones, interrupting.

Mario looked dangerous. Would he revert to type
and attack? Bones looked about him for a weapon,
noting a heavy vase near at hand. But Mario did not
attack. He merely sneered and rose to get himself a
drink, not offering Bones one.

Bones had had enough. He turned and started for
the door.

"Did I say I was through talking?" yelled Mario.

"That was my understanding," said Bones. "You
said you were going to handle it. I'll take care of Willie
and the boys."

Mario fell down into a chair and sat staring, drink
in hand. Bones observed him for a moment, then went
out. It wasn't worth it. It just wasn't worth it.

◆§

BUT BEFORE HE GOT BACK to the hotel; he was having
second thoughts. This might well mean the end of
Mario, or his triumph. If the former, Bones would stay
on; if the latter, Bones would bow out, or there would
have to be different arrangements made if The Man
wanted to continue to use his services.

It would really be foolish to kick away thousands of dollars out of pique. But Bones decided to protect himself by doing something unprecedented: calling The Man. Nobody called The Man. It was impossible to get him. The Man did the calling. All the same, Bones had an emergency number and this, in his opinion, was an emergency.

The assistant manager of the hotel where the party was being held very deferentially ushered Bones to a private office at the back where he could, as the assistant manager said, phone at his ease.

The Man came on at once. "Mac? What the hell?"

Bones quickly outlined the interview and The Man laughed. "I told the dago to handle it, didn't I? So let him handle it." Bones heard The Man laughing, then the connection was broken.

Bones didn't know what to think. But he felt relief at one manifestation. He hadn't annoyed The Man by calling. If he was annoyed, you knew it—and heard about it, sometimes at length. Was this the end of Mario? Was The Man, a real smart bastard, aware of it?

Good feelings began to well up in William as he crossed the big, ornate lobby to the banquet room, where the table had been removed and now there was dancing. Daphne was dancing with big Ben Mosely, who was wearing a red, white, and blue Uncle Sam hat. Daphne's eyes lit up at the sight of William.

"Well, that was quick," she said.

"Oh, it was just next door. And we tycoons make those momentous decisions very fast. Right, Ben?"

"Right or wrong, very fast," said Ben; then: "Take her, William. I'm a lousy dancer and she's just putting up with me because I'm Irma's husband."

So William and Daphne waltzed to a string version of "Underneath The Stars," and for the time being at least it seemed like a possible world after all to William.

*

THIS WAS A very uncomfortable time for the non-straight johns of Chicago. Murtaugh, of the Metropolitan Hoodlum Squad, didn't run just one dragnet, he ran one every night for five consecutive nights, and hundreds of hoods were now on the scatter. And Murtaugh was not only slamming them into the tanks, he was vagging them. If they had no visible means of support they were charged with vagrancy, a misdemeanor, and forced to make bail or stay in clink. The vagging was a deliberate type of police harassment that the CPD resorted to when from time to time they got sick and tired of the proliferation of hoodlums all over the city. And the hoods, a tough lot, were not handled with kid gloves by any means—one smart crack out of one of them and he got slammed in the mouth and kicked around. The tanks were full of protesting hoods. Many couldn't get through to anybody. Some guys with a thousand dollars or more in their billfolds were vagged and held over for trial; of course they could at least make bail. Downtown was a bedlam, with complaining and even whining hoods who couldn't make an outside contact—the raids were usually conducted after midnight—and were forced to sleep on cots in corridors or even in some cases on the floor.

Even Fatso managed to get himself picked up and vagged, but he had money in his pocket and could at least make bail after a night stretch in the tank.

It got so bad that around the station at times there were more bail bondsmen than police.

Worst of all from the standpoint of the hoods, many wanted men were picked up—some of them badly wanted, including a couple of escaped murderers.

Several civil groups began to protest, and there was even an article in one of the papers complaining about "abuse of police power," but Murtaugh ignored all this, and he was backed up by Sluggo, the lieutenant. It did the hearts of many police good to see the hoods dragged in and at least inconvenienced. They were an arrogant lot who gave the police and everybody else nothing but trouble, and the police considered their value to society to be nil.

But the most-wanted hood of all did not turn up in the net—Ted Beck. He seemed to have vanished. Murtaugh's special detail couldn't find him anyplace, or get a lead, and it was the same with the special deputies, Fiore and Maxon, from the Southwest Precinct— Krumpacker's boys.

Meanwhile the turmoil continued in the city, and hoods began to hole up and hide—either that or leave town. Many ran into friends in Detroit, Toledo, Gary, and Milwaukee. There were many hood reunions in unlikely places. And as the exodus grew, police in the various cities of exile began to feel the weight of a new presence in their communities; crimes of violence took a sudden and startling jump upward.

But with Ted, the most sought-after hood of all, things were quiet, and he'd become reconciled to his hermitlike existence, at least for the time being. He went to bed late and slept late. He played solitaire, listened to the radio around the clock—it was always on—and in general managed to compose himself. He never went out except very late at night and then only when he needed supplies. There was a twenty-four-hour market only six blocks away, and he always took his car; not only because it was safer but to give the car a little work: otherwise it would just be sitting there rusting away. Not once had he noticed anything suspicious. Nobody paid any attention to him as he went around in the dress of the place: an open-necked shirt and dark pants. In this area nobody wore coats or ties. And Ted's car was cheap and nondescript, not the kind that would be noticed; in fact the car fit right into the neighborhood.

Sometimes in the evening he would hear the people next door talking; the renovation had been ramshackle, the walls thin. They were a middle-aged couple and seemed to spend most of their time quarreling —but not loudly, no yelling; just constant bickering. On the other side was a young couple who always seemed to be away.

Two Polish families with kids lived upstairs, and they were very noisy, stamping overhead. Often Ted would hear them in the hallway, talking Polish in loud voices, and Ted was surprised that he could understand practically every word they said. He hadn't uttered a word of Polish since he was sixteen years old and had run away from home, out into the non-Polish world he preferred.

His grandfather hardly ever talked about anything at all but Cracow. And Ted's father hated the USA, hated Chicago, and saved his money like a miser to go back to Poland, where he'd been born. Go back he did, but the grandfather had died before it was possible. Ted had two sisters someplace; hadn't heard from them in years but they were probably still in Chicago, maybe in the same old neighborhood. Ted had no desire to see them. He'd always been considered a kind of black sheep, a changeling in the nest of a respectable Polish family.

It was late, going on two A.M. Ted was eating a sandwich and playing solitaire, and just beyond him the radio hummed on. Half the time Ted hardly listened to it, was just vaguely conscious of what was being conveyed, but it was company; anything was better than constant silence, especially at night. He began to feel drowsy and decided that after he finished this game he'd hit the sack a little earlier than usual. He hadn't slept well the night before, possibly due to the large amount of Polish sausage he'd eaten. He'd forgotten how good it was, the food of his childhood, and he couldn't stop eating it. But his stomach was now used to blander fare, and he'd felt slightly queasy ever since.

He nodded off, he didn't know for how long. But suddenly he was jerked awake by the sound of heavy footfalls in the hallway. This was very unusual. Ted turned off the radio and got out his guns; to his .38 he'd added a heavy-duty .45 Colt revolver he'd picked up in a gun store. Then he paused. Somebody was banging on the door of the young couple down the hall. They kept banging but got no response.

He heard somebody say: "He's in there all right. He wouldn't go away and leave his car."

The banging continued. Finally Ted heard somebody coming down the stairs, disturbed by the racket, and a voice with a heavy Polish accent demanded: "Hey, what you man do down there?"

"We're looking for Ted Beck."

"Hey, why you bang and knock so? You policeman?"

"Yeah," said a heavy voice.

"I don't know no Beck. No Beck here."

"Tall guy with curly blond hair."

"No Mr. Beck. That's Mr. Panov. You got mix-up, Officer."

"Yeah, okay, Pop," said the heavy voice.

While the conversation was going on, Ted was both listening and considering the situation. It was a trap, no doubt about it. They knew about his car, so somebody was staked there. And if he made a run for it out the window, the man at the car had him. If he didn't he was dead anyway. Pretty neat. Only one little slipup—they'd hit the wrong apartment in this crazy warren and tipped off the victim.

Ted's car was parked in the alley behind the house, so his window on the hill side was clear. If a guy had the car staked out, he couldn't see the window. Fine.

So Ted listened, tense. "Right down there," he heard the Polish voice say. "That door."

Ted heard them coming, big heavy-footed guys, hoods, no doubt. He clipped on his .38 and carrying the .45 in his hand, he slipped out the window just as the knocking started. Keeping to the wall, he slid along the house and cautiously peered around the corner. There was the guy, staked out not by the car but above it on a kind of terrace, hardly ten feet away from Ted, and Ted was on top of him before he was aware that anything was happening. Ted pistol-whipped him with the .45 and the guy fell with a despairing groan and rolled down the terrace into the alley, taking a very hard fall. Now Ted crept back along the house. They were just kicking in his door. He'd left the lights on, so they would soon be in the light while he was in the dark outside. Barely moving, not making a sound, he inched toward the window and peered in.

Strangers to Ted, but hoods all right, that was plain. Both were big and tough-looking. "He blew fast," said one. "Looka this sandwich, half-ate."

"Maybe Birdie's got him by now."

"Yeah."

Ted rose suddenly and through the window shot them both. They pitched around, grabbing the furniture, and one began to yell in anguish. Then they both fell in a tangle and finally rolled apart. There was hardly ever any reply to a .45 at short range.

Ted had been living out of his suitcases. It was no problem to strap them up, and in a couple of minutes he was in and out the window. The stakeout guy was lying very still. Ted stepped over him, got into his car, and drove off.

Lights were beginning to come on all over the neighborhood. A .45 makes a very loud bang.

Ted followed the alley to the next cross street and was just turning onto it when he heard the police siren. A car was coming very fast. He noted a dark filling station and quickly ducked into it and parked his car in one of the stalls and cut his lights. The radio car ripped past, its siren screaming, and turned up Ted's street. The upstairs Pole had probably called the cops.

Ted eased out of the filling station, drove to the corner, paused, and looked up the street. Sure enough, the radio car had stopped at Ted's former address.

After hesitating for a moment Ted turned and drove south. Where now? Well, deeper into his old territory. Where else?

And as he drove along through the deserted streets of a working-class neighborhood, he kept wondering who the strange hoods had been. He'd expected Willie, Fatso, Steve, and Zell, or two of them at least. Why had strangers been hired? Had the four of them got bounced because Ted had managed to get away? It was the only answer he could think of.

❧

BONES WAITED, first at his downtown office, then at his apartment; he felt disinclined to go out and face the world in general. What in the hell was going on? The Maria case and its ramifications had been buried in the depths of the papers, but this one had hit the headlines and even extras were being hawked through the streets. Huge black type read: GANG WAR FLARES AGAIN: TWO SLAIN, ONE DYING. And it turned out that all three were big-time hoods: Attilio Bruno and Tough Gus Retz were the dead; the dying was Art "Birdie" Shay. Attilio Bruno, it said further, was also known as the Sharpshooter. Bones felt certain these were the "bird dogs" sent out by Mario. And Mario had been right, in a way; they had found Ted, no doubt about that!

Bones felt shaky. It was so easy to misjudge a man. He'd known that Ted was a former hood, but he had put him in a lower classification altogether. How had he managed to knock them all out of action? Fantastic!

Bones seldom if ever questioned his own judgment. Now he couldn't help bring it under examination. If he could be so wrong about Ted, he could be wrong about anything, everything, and he was in a situation where errors of judgment could be very costly indeed.

The day passed. He heard nothing from anybody. Why didn't Mario call? Why, for that matter, didn't The Man call?

Finally Bones couldn't stand the disturbing inaction any longer, so he set up a meeting with Kemper. At least he would be doing or appear to be doing something.

They met at Kemper's overfurnished but strictly lower middle-class apartment on the Southwest Side. Kemper was no Ted. He was not one for elegance or what he called putting on the dog; in fact elegance disturbed him, made him uncomfortable. He lived for cheap, as Willie said, and his new status made no difference to him in that respect.

On the other hand Bones felt uncomfortable in Kemper's habitat. Bones had come from a monied family and had always lived as most other Americans did not live—that is, expensively. In fact he'd always taken it for granted until he'd come to Chicago as a youngish lawyer and had quickly found out how the "other half" lived. Nothing was more repugnant to Bones than the endlessly stretching drab suburbs of Chicago. Most of the time he managed to blot all awareness of them from his consciousness: he moved from an elegant small office to expensive and so-called exclusive eating places to an elegant apartment. But at the moment he was right in the middle of this drabness and talking on familiar terms with one of its typical denizens.

As Kemper had been working on the books all day, he was still wearing his green eyeshade. He was very proud of his work and got out his latest ledger for Bones to study. In his time Bones had studied many a ledger and was adept at reading one, and Kemper's was a model. A valuable man, no doubt about it—but not as boss of an operation like this. Bones sat worrying. Would he have to take it over himself? And he made up his mind that if he didn't hear from Mario or The Man within a reasonable length of time, that was just what he would do. Willie he could count on. And he was sure Willie could handle the hoods.

He tried to talk policy with Kemper, but he was wasting his time. Kemper kept going back to the books, the new accounting system he had set up, the increased profits, the many ways he was dreaming up to cut expenses, some of them very impractical. This was a strange business, not like other businesses. You were dealing in people, not product. In his mind Kemper was dealing in product.

Bones decided Kemper simply wouldn't do, and suddenly he found himself regretting Ted's huge "dummy" that had gotten them into all this trouble. It was obvious, now that he was gone, that Ted had been a very valuable man who knew his business and left the bookkeeping to the likes of Kemper.

As an accountant, Kemper was invaluable and would have to be retained; as a boss, he might turn out to be a disaster.

Later Bones had a long talk with Willie, warning him to keep a very sharp eye on Kemper till Bones had made up his mind just what was best to do.

Willie nodded slowly. "He's an all-right guy," said Willie, "but he don't know what he's doing."

Then they talked about Ted. Willie just sat shaking his head. "He really took care of them monkeys," said Willie. "I was wise he knew his way around, but. . . . So what do we do?"

"I'm waiting for word," said Bones. "We were called off."

Willie laughed sardonically. "Yeah," he said. "Maybe they done us a favor. The word around is that the Southwest bulls are after him."

"That could be," said Bones, straight-faced.

⋅≼§

THE EVENING PASSED. Bones went out for a quick lonely dinner, then hurried back to his apartment. About nine o'clock The Man called. He seemed in an odd mood. Bones had the disquieting feeling that he was being laughed at. And strangely enough The Man made no mention of Mario or of the killings.

"How's it going over in the Southwest, Mac?" asked The Man.

Bones explained all about the meeting.

"Fine," said The Man. "Hang in there. But don't make no changes . . . yet . . . not till you hear from me."

Then The Man talked about another one of his successful gambling forays and hung up rather abruptly, or so it seemed to Bones.

Bones felt worried, shaken, upset—what was going on? This was unnatural; grotesque, even. Here Mario had pulled a terrible "dummy" and The Man had not even made one reference to it. And Bones had the feeling all through the conversation that The Man was secretly amused—but at whose expense? Normally you'd expect a goof like Mario and his bird dogs to make him furious—and when he got furious, men ran for cover. But, no; The Man just seemed to be passing the time of day.

Bones sat trying to read, waiting for the phone to ring. Certainly Mario would call; but he didn't. And in view of their final scene together, Bones couldn't bring himself to call M-6. He'd just have to sweat it out.

ALL WAS TURMOIL and uncertainty in the shadow world as the dragnets seemed to be off, for the time being at least, and the hoods kept drifting back from Detroit, Milwaukee, Gary, Toledo, and other points of the compass. They began turning up in their usual haunts, but warily, and trying to be guided in their conduct by news from the grapevine that kept flooding in. But this wasn't the usual grapevine; this was one, two, three grapevines, with contradictory information. The truth of the matter was that nobody seemed to know what was going on.

Who could believe that guys like Birdie, the Sharpshooter, and Tough Gus could be taken like that? And by that Polack Ted Beck, or whatever his name was! It couldn't be. The consensus seemed to be that the truth just was not appearing in the papers. Beck must have had help.

Ted Beck had been positively identified now as the killer, from Bertillon pictures shown to his fellow tenants, who had known him as John Panov (a family name).

In the dives now many guys who never read anything were reading the papers, trying to get a lead, an angle, trying to figure if the heat was coming back so they could be prepared this time. The dragnet routine, the vagging, was bad, boy, bad! It really interfered with your life-style, and oh them Murtaugh bulls were tough! It wasn't right, cops playing like that. It was unconstitutional. One newspaper even said so.

JOE FELT WORRIED and confused as the extras kept hitting the street and the wildest kinds of rumors continued to run through the police department. There had even been an article in a tabloid damning the police and claiming that the crime commission would soon release a report showing widespread corruption in the CPD.

But there was nothing but silence, at least at the Northwest Precinct, in regard to the Maria Ricordi matter and its connection with the most wanted man in the city, Ted Beck. Annoyed, Joe felt that at times everybody was leaning over backward to be nice to him—even Lieutenant Janowicz.

But of course a tabloid had grabbed the story and done a piece about CPD Sergeant Joseph P. Ricordi, his wife Maria, and her unexplained connection with the "killer," Taddeus Byscznski, alias Ted Beck. There were even veiled implications that somehow Sergeant Ricordi was involved in some illegitimate way not stated. Joe was white with anger when he read the article, but he soon calmed himself. This tabloid largely published unmitigated trash and was generally held in contempt in the city.

But at Dom's apartment all was serene. Tabloids were never allowed to penetrate that pleasant domain, and Joe, on his last visit, had found the kids happy and healthy and even tanned from many visits to the beach.

It was Dom's day off and he had cooked the dinner himself, with antipasto, soup, and a delicious entree of veal that the kids couldn't get enough of, and for dessert Neapolitan ice cream. Joe ate more than usual and felt very tight around the waist, but the kids had out-eaten him. It always amazed him, the food that little kids could store away without apparent damage to their anatomies. They'd finally had to make young Joe stop eating the ice cream after two extra helpings.

Joe sat back, smoked a rare cigar, and looked all about him. Too bad most homes were not this happy and well run. Dom had married just the right woman, and Paula just the right man, and Joe sat thinking how lucky he was to have a place like this for his motherless kids. He paid, of course, in spite of Dom's objections that he was making four or five times as much as Joe, maybe more. But Joe would have it no other way.

Joe, Jr. and Maria had shown very little attention to him, but Joe was getting used to that now. He was their father, of course, and they accepted him as that, but he was also just a man who appeared once a week or less and interrupted their ordinary way of life by his presence. They always seemed to be self-consciously on their good behavior, not free and easy as with Dom and Paula. In the past Joe had had occasional twinges of jealousy, but now he was more inclined to accept the situation and thank God that he'd been able to solve one of his major problems so easily. As for remarrying, giving them a stepmother . . . well, he wouldn't think of it. One marriage was enough. That it had ended in disaster was due to something stronger than himself: the will of God, what else?

Another marriage, another house, another family could lead to nothing but unhappiness and confusion, in Joe's opinion, and he had made up his mind that he would live celibate the rest of his life, as he had for the last three years. Others might think it was unnatural.

Priests did not; nor did Joe. Without love, sex meant nothing to Joe. He had always been that way.

As a teenager and a very young adult, it had manifested itself in the romanticism that some of the girls had found so funny. They were used to being grabbed and pinched; they were used to assaults on their virtue. They were not used to Joe's polite and sometimes worshipful approach.

After dinner, while the kids listened to a favorite radio program in another room, Joe, Dom, and Paula talked, desultorily, mere chatter, but pleasant . . . about St. Martin's and the new social activities there, about movies, about the weather, about the wonderful fireworks display they had taken the kids to see at the beach . . . just the trivia of life, the things that were so lacking in Joe's hard existence.

Dom and Paula stayed off the subject of the police, of crime, of anything that had to do with what they secretly spoke of as Joe's cross. Joe's cross had always been Helga, what else? And yet it had been far from a total loss. Look at Joe, Jr. and Maria—bright, healthy kids, doing fine in school and getting along very well with everybody. No problem. At least no problem to Dom and Paula, who did not expect too much and were easily pleased. They were not perfectionists, far from it, and that was one reason they were so happy and why things in general went so smoothly for them.

"Father Pasquale was asking about you Sunday, Joe," said Paula. "You ought to go more often."

"I know," said Joe contritely.

"Yes, he should go," said Dom. "But he also needs all the rest he can get. Look how thin he is!"

"Haven't lost a pound," said Joe.

"Well . . . you look thin. Don't he, Paula?"

"Yes," said Paula. "You should come and have Dom cook for you more often." That was Paula's way. To turn everything off with a joke, make light of it.

So . . . sitting now in his own living room, smoking and listening to the radio after dinner at Dom's, he was feeling a little more mellow than usual, and far less tense. It was a very pleasant night, warm but not hot, with a lake breeze occasionally stirring his curtains. He thought of the past, of his first days with Maria, of the kids when they were babies, happy little nuisances who used to keep them up at night, of trips to the dunes, of boat rides, of pulling them on sleds across icy Chicago streets, and of Christmases with trees and toys . . . and he never once thought of the ugly present, of what had really happened to Maria, or of the most wanted man in town, Ted Beck.

A quick tapping at his door brought him suddenly back to reality. Dave? But to his surprise it was Gina, alone. In fact he was so surprised that he just stood and stared at her for a moment.

"Can't I come in?" asked Gina, who seemed very disturbed.

"Yes," said Joe, coming to. "Come in."

Gina hurried in and sank into a chair. "Can I have a drink? Wine? Anything."

Joe poured her a glass of his Chianti and she took a long swallow. "That dirty bum . . . that old pal of yours. You know what he did? He took my money—five hundred dollars . . ." cried Gina, her black eyes blazing. "So I said to myself, I'll just go and tell Joe what a bum his old pal is."

Joe sat down opposite her. "Johnny stole your money?" Somehow it didn't sound right. "When did this happen?"

"Just now," cried Gina. "And then he went to the bathroom to take a shower and I ran out. He took my money. A certified check for five hundred dollars and he wouldn't give it back. He's always grabbing my letters . . . he's a bum, a bum—and he'll never be anything else."

"You mean somebody sent you a check for five hundred dollars?"

"Yes, that's what I'm telling you," cried Gina. "Mr. Everett. He sent me this certified check for five hundred dollars and he said I could use it to come to Paris if I want to."

"Do you want to?"

"Yes," cried Gina. "Of course I want to. And here this bum grabs it and won't give it back. Well . . . he doesn't own me, even if he thinks he does."

"Maybe he was only kidding you, Gina."

Gina stared at Joe blankly for a moment, then she said: "Oh, no. He's just afraid I'll go to Paris. He's always making cracks about Mr. Everett . . . that he's a pansy and that he paints stupid pictures and that he talks funny . . . and . . . well, you've heard him . . ."

There was a pounding at the door. Joe was beginning to get damned annoyed, and when he opened the door and confronted Johnny, his face was hard, his eyes unfriendly. He did not like to have his apartment used as a kind of playground or convenience.

But Johnny ignored or more likely didn't even notice Joe's attitude, and roaring with laughter, he pointed a finger at Gina and said: "Sucker! I knew you'd run right over here." Johnny broke himself up laughing.

"Now listen, Johnny," Joe began, his voice hard, but all at once Gina began to cry and sob.

"Oh, you stupid sonofabitch," she sobbed. "You are driving me crazy."

Johnny sobered up at once. "Hey, none of that. Here. Here's your lousy check. I was only kidding you. Here, stupid. Put it in your purse."

Gina stopped sobbing and looked at Johnny reproachfully. Then she snatched the check out of his hand and put it away. "You're such a fool," she said. "You think Joe wants us breaking in here over some silly ape's idea of a joke? I'm sorry, Joe. I thought he meant it. I won't let him fool me again like that. I'm sorry."

"It's okay," said Joe; then to Johnny: "You dumb bastard, what's the matter with you? Why don't you grow up? You think you're still back in high school? I remember all your gags and tricks. Well . . . stop it! You're forty years old."

"You better look out," said Johnny, "or I'll wrassle you."

Joe turned away in disgust, but Johnny came over and put his arm around him. "Come on, Joe. Relax, for once. Who are you, the king of the Mounties? Where's your red coat?"

That even made Joe laugh, so he got out the wine bottle and they sat down at the table.

"And I'm going to Paris," said Gina, "and see the Eiffel Tower and the Louvre museum and the Folly Bergere and all those artist places Mr. Everett wrote me about and . . ."

"Send Joe and me back some dirty postcards, will you, Gina?" said Johnny.

"You think I'm kidding, don't you? Well, I'm not. I'm going, and you can't stop me."

"Did I say anything about stopping you? You flatter

yourself. You are beginning to bore me. You have no more mysteries for me, like I heard a guy say in the movies. I need a fresh broad."

"Oh, sure," said Gina. "That's not what you say at night."

For once Johnny was stopped. And Joe enjoyed his embarrassment. He kept laughing, and finally Johnny joined in.

"Well," he said, "I gotta admit . . ."

"Oh, shut up," said Gina.

About half an hour later they left, arguing and bickering. And Joe sat on, sipping his wine. Whether he would admit it or not, Johnny and Gina had given him a breather. They had distracted him, afforded him nearly an hour of respite. And as he sipped his wine, every once in a while he'd laugh to himself about how Gina had brought Johnny up short and the look on Johnny's face.

&§

THE TWO GUYS in the radio car, Sam Jones, a black, and Carl Wetzel, had just about had it. It was a Saturday night and they had run into nothing but trouble. Both were rookies, which was very unusual in itself; rookies were almost never teamed up together. But manpower was in short supply and the CPD just had to do the best it could.

Sam was driving, Carl slumped down trying to relax. Their problem hadn't been crime but just ordinary citizens. Two bar fights; trouble in a big crowded restaurant, where Sam had gotten slammed against a table by a fat patron who for the moment was out of hand because he insisted he'd been overcharged. And

Carl had pushed the fat guy's arm up behind him till the guy actually cried, big tears. And then there had been a family fight of such proportions and so many ramifications that Sam and Carl had had to break it up three different times. Family fights were the worst. Sometimes both sides turned on the police.

Sam had torn up his knuckles against the table and had a handkerchief wrapped around his hand.

"Saturday night!" said Carl, with feeling.

"Yeah," said Sam. "In my neighborhood we have it big! The guys work all week and get ginned up on Saturday night. Trouble, man!"

"In the academy we didn't hear too much about Saturday night."

"No, man, we didn't," said Sam. "That book stuff looks different once you get out."

"Did you see that big blond woman try to bite me?"

Sam leaned against the wheel to laugh, remembering Carl hopping away frantically from the enraged woman.

Suddenly Sam stopped laughing; he had noticed something up ahead.

"We got trouble," he said, and Carl groaned.

Half a block up something was going on in the parking lot of a supermarket; they could see people running toward the lot from all directions, and strangely enough, some running away from it; and cars were pulling both in and out.

"What they got here, a carnival or something?" cried Sam, stepping on it a little.

But things were so congested that Sam couldn't get into the parking lot, and he touched his siren. People turned, stared, then there was a wild hubbub. "The cops, the cops."

Sam pulled the car into the lot, and little by little the

crowd drew back from it till the two rookies could see up ahead of them a strange tableau: a guy had apparently fallen out of a car and was lying face down on the cement, with one foot still grotesquely in the car, and close to him stood a dark, stocky, heavy-shouldered man in a short-sleeved yellow T-shirt, with a blunt-looking automatic weapon across his forearm; and beyond him was another guy, a blond guy with a short haircut, a shotgun in his hands, warily watching the crowd.

Sam pulled to a stop, and people began to crowd around them, talking and protesting and pointing, but there was such a hubbub the two rookies could make nothing out of what was being said till one large, middle-aged woman put her head in the window and yelled: "They shot him. He just got out of his car and they shot him. . . ."

The rookies exchanged a long look. They had small arms; these guys had a shotgun and an automatic weapon. It was a problem. What did the book say about that?

They got out of the car cautiously, the mere sight of their uniforms quieting the crowd to some extent; and remembering their training, they moved slowly toward the trouble spot, widely separated.

The guy in the yellow shirt gestured to them abruptly to come, to hurry. Sam approached him, while Carl, far to his right, cautiously kept his distance, and yet he was in good revolver range.

The guy in the yellow shirt whipped out a wallet and handed it to Sam. Inside was a CPD badge, and Sam read on the card: Detective Sergeant Ezio Fiore: S-D (special detail). Sam turned and nodded to Carl, then gave back the wallet.

"Get these people off our backs," said Fiore; then he

turned to the blond guy. "You can go call in now, Fred."

Maxon gestured and went pushing his way through the crowd. Carl joined Sam and together they moved slowly among the people, who were calming down now, assuring them everything was okay, it was a police matter, not to worry, just keep moving, go on about their business . . . But the large, middle-aged woman still kept insisting: "They shot him. He just got out of his car and they shot him . . ." She seemed slightly hysterical, so Sam and Carl ignored her.

Fiore rolled the body over and took two guns from inside the man's coat: a .38 and a .45. The people stared and exclaimed. One of them grabbed the middle-aged woman and pointed this out to her. She stared, then began to cry and sob, and finally a young girl came hurriedly and took charge of her.

"Mom," said the girl, "I've been looking for you everyplace."

"They just shot him," said the woman. "It was terrible." She was led away sobbing.

Sam was speechless now that things had quieted down. He took out a handkerchief and mopped his brow. Cold sweat! Oh, man, could they have made a mistake! In his mind Sam had dubbed Sergeant Fiore a hoodlum. Good thing he didn't act on the assumption.

Maxon returned. "Morgue wagon's on the way." Then he examined the .45. "Well, maybe this'll clear up a couple of shootings."

"So . . . ?" said Fiore.

Sam and Carl, their work accomplished, didn't know what to do, stay or leave, and the dicks seemed to be paying no attention to them.

Finally Sam called: "You need us, Sergeant?"

"Yeah," said Fiore. "Stick around. We need the uniforms."

Maxon laughed curtly. Sam and Carl exchanged a look, then they returned to the radio car, got in, and sat waiting. Although both were badly shaken, this at least was a respite. After a moment Carl got out his pad and began to sketch the report he'd later have to write and turn in.

"Man!" said Sam.

Carl turned and looked at him.

"I almost made one big mistake," said Sam.

"Yeah," said Carl. "I was thinking the same thing."

Time passed. Finally they heard the ding-a-ling of the morgue wagon and watched while the body was unceremoniously tossed onto a stretcher and dumped into the back.

Then Sam got out and crossed over to Fiore. "Need us anymore?"

Fiore didn't even look at him. He seemed preoccupied. "No. Go on."

"Nice friendly guy," said Sam, as he got back into the radio car and drove off.

Static began to buzz on their radio, then a call came over. A row at an all-night grocery store. Sam and Carl exchanged looks but made no comment.

❧

THE RINGING of the phone pulled Joe out of an uneasy sleep. He switched on the light and glanced at his wristwatch on the night table. After two A.M. Trouble? What kind? Half-asleep, nervous, he felt very apprehensive . . . and then surprised, as it turned out to be the nightman, Sergeant O'Brien, at the Northwest Precinct.

"Joe? Sorry to wake you up," said O'Brien. "But word just came through. Two police officers shot and killed Ted Beck in a supermarket on the South Side."

Silence.

"Joe? Are you there?"

"Are they sure?"

"We got the word—positive identification. Just thought . . . well, just thought you wouldn't want to wait till tomorrow to . . ."

Joe couldn't take it in.

"Thanks, Frank. Many thanks," said Joe, feeling stunned, disoriented.

He went into the living room, lit a cigarette, and sat in the dark, thinking. It was a very warm night, breathless. And the stillness seemed to throb in the street outside. So . . . it was all over. Joe was like a man who had been carrying an almost unbearable burden, only to find it suddenly and unexpectedly lifted from his shoulders, and immediately the world took on a different aspect. Contrary impulses tugged at Joe. He didn't know what to do—dance, sing, weep, or get out his accordion. Thank God he had acted with good sense—against his deepest instincts to strike, to strike back.

Little by little all tension left his body. He felt limp, almost groggy. He had been keyed to such a pitch for so long that the reaction was extreme. In a moment, like a sleepwalker, he returned to the bedroom and just fell into bed. He felt a strong desire to sleep, to blot out the world, to sleep for a very long time.

What would have been Joe's reaction if he'd known the truth of the matter? In Joe's mind the picture was a simple one: the abominable guilt of Ted Beck and the innocence of Maria. And yet in this matter Ted Beck had been guilty only of bad judgment, his downfall coming only because an employee had bungled a simple assignment, while no objective person could consider Maria innocent. No force had been used on her. She was an adult, doing as she pleased, fully responsible, legally and otherwise, for her actions.

Could Joe ever have absorbed such a truth if it had been presented to him with all the details? It's very unlikely. We believe what we want or what we are compelled to believe, by our nature and by our circumstances. Each man has his own "truth"; and that is why even men who speak the same language seldom understand each other. They are talking about two different things.

Would Joe have been better off if he had known the truth? That is even more doubtful. No is probably the true answer. Some men can't bear to hear the unadorned truth, and Joe had always been a romantic, though he was unaware of it. There were times when Joe was very puzzled when he became suddenly aware that his view of things seemed so different from the views of others. Were they dumb? Perverse? Or what?

But at the moment Joe was not worrying about anything. He was sleeping heavily as the night wore on. The moon slid below the horizon, and faint tinges of gray began to appear in the sky over the near North Side rooftops.

❧

BONES HAD BEEN to a dinner party out in Lake Forest with Daphne, and as he hadn't got to bed till nearly three A.M., he was still asleep at eleven in the morning. What seemed like vague shouting woke him. His windows were wide open, and it was already very hot. Another scorcher, probably. The shouting seemed to diminish, die away altogether; then another, a newer voice, took up the cry and finally he got it: "Extra! Extra! Extra!"

Bones rose and went to get the paper that appeared outside his door every morning, courtesy of the management. But it was an early edition with no scare heads, and he was just about to call down for an extra when the phone rang. It was The Man.

"Heard the news?" asked The Man.

"Out late. Just got up."

The Man chuckled. "Well," he said, "you're my man. A couple of Krumpacker's boys turned the trick."

"Beck?"

"Right. And now the train's on the track. I've just been waiting. The whole operation was getting completely out of hand, getting too big for the way it was run. I've set it up different. But with this silly bastard loose . . . well . . . ever hear of The Tangerine, the big restaurant on the West Side?"

"No," said Bones, wondering, a little nervous; he wasn't really sure of anything The Man was saying.

So at a command from The Man, Bones got out his fountain pen and wrote down an address, with precise instructions on where to park, how to enter.

Then The Man said: "I bought out the whole place, through a stooge, of course, and now it's ours. Great front for the operation. It'll have everything, all in one place. Maury Degnan will meet you there and explain things . . ."

Maury Degnan! Bones couldn't believe his ears. The Man and Maury had fought each other for years, all over the North Side.

"Maury Degnan?" Bones couldn't keep the surprise out of his voice.

The Man laughed. "Tough Irish bastard. I almost got him once. Don't know how many times he almost got me. Well . . . what the hell! You check with Maury . . ."

Bones felt confused.

"And . . . Mac," The Man went on after a silence: "No part of management for you, understand? I just want your mind, your legal ability—your advice—and your clout at Southwest. Maybe I'll jump the check up a little, okay? Though God knows you're clipping me for plenty as it is!"

Bones had a feeling he was being eased out, all power removed from his hands—and yet was that a bad thing? It was not, as long as the money kept rolling in . . . and as long as he was useful and didn't pull a dummy.

"Just check with Maury," said The Man. "Talk to you later. Wait a minute. Same proprietors will run The Tangerine, as if there'd been no sale. Smooth, right?" The Man hung up laughing, leaving dozens of question marks hanging in the air.

Bones sent down for an extra, stared at the black headlines, and read the account of the killing of Ted Beck by Southwest Precinct dicks Ezio Fiore and Frederick Maxon. However, according to the paper, reactions were mixed. Some deplored the killing, others said the two Chicago officers should be given medals. But none of this mattered, as Bones well knew. It would all be forgotten in a day or two, with the news-

papers turning to other matters, to other sensations—
of which Chicago was full; and when Chicago failed
to oblige, the newspaper writers would whip up something themselves or revive and refurbish an earlier
sensation. In Europe everybody thought if you came
from Chicago you were a gangster or at least a friend
of gangsters, all this, courtesy of the US press, which
was hysterical over Chicago and its gangsters, who
really were, Bones knew, a sorry lot.

Bones put the paper aside and sat lost in thought for
a while. He was as yet far from sure of The Man's
intentions: and not one word about Mario—and
where did Maury Degnan fit in, a real hoodlum and
leader of hoodlums? Was more muscle needed? What
was the point . . . ?

Bones kept wondering about Mario, and finally he
couldn't stand the suspense any longer, his curiosity
nagging at him and even little fears running around
at the back of his mind, so he called Mario's private
number, direct line. After no answer and a brief delay,
he was informed by an operator that the phone had
been disconnected. Bones thought this over for a moment, then he called the switchboard at Mario's hotel
and was informed that "Mr. Fanelli is no longer with
us."

What did it mean? That Mario had moved to the
West Side and had his new headquarters at The Tangerine? Or did it mean that Mario had pulled one
dummy too many?

This took thought. You don't buy out a place like
The Tangerine overnight, nor do you hire Maury
Degnan to work for you out of the blue. All this had
taken preparation by The Man; planning, even long-
range planning. Had the Ted Beck dummy happened

at just the wrong time, followed by Mario's dummy in getting his killers killed? Bones remembered he'd noted more than once that there was something odd about The Man's attitude. Did this explain it?

Bones felt he was right about this, and now Ted Beck's death had opened the whole matter up. It wasn't so much the Maria affair that was bad, but the fact that if Murtaugh had laid his hands on Ted Beck, Ted might have been more than willing to spill the whole operation, or as much as he knew of it, in order to make a deal and maybe plead guilty to a lesser charge . . . or maybe even be given immunity.

If this were true, then Bones was in a solid position, even if management power was taken away from him. Management wasn't his métier anyway; he'd only gotten involved because Mario had wanted him involved, maybe out of slackness, indifference; Bones's forte was advice, legal and otherwise, and pull.

Bones decided he'd be lazy for the day, so he showered, put on fresh pajamas, and had his breakfast sent up. Occasionally now a breeze blew in from the lake, stirring the curtains. Bones called his office and said he wouldn't be in; his office was hardly more than a blind anyway, although he occasionally had clients. They were almost always moneyed people, usually with money problems of some kind, from how to hide assets to how to keep their income tax down, though God knows they paid little as it was. But any at all was anathema to some of the people he dealt with, most of whom thought the USA was going to some kind of socialistic hell . . . but all were coining money.

The stock market kept going up, and the papers daily informed their readers all about the country's unprecedented prosperity, with the implication that it wasn't even a drop in the bucket as yet. Even the elevator men and secretaries were in the market now. Speculation had become a way of life. But Bones was wary of it, and though he occasionally dabbled in the market, he never got in over his head. It was never sink or swim by any means; small losses he could stand.

There were times late at night when Bones would study his life in Chicago with clear eyes and wonder. How long could it last? Not forever, that was for sure. A tide of opposition was rising on all sides—to crime, to Prohibition, to the arrogant gangsters, to police corruption, to a whole way of life. When and how the crash would come Bones wasn't sure, but come it would. Everything was getting out of hand.

And yet . . . he couldn't quite bring himself to take what he'd won and go. Go where? Certainly not back to Detroit and his snobbish and hidebound relatives in Grosse Pointe. New York? But he knew no one in New York. Start from scratch in that huge overblown jungle? How would he begin? No, Chicago was now his home. So . . . what's to do?

Bones sat wondering about Mario as he ate his breakfast and looked out at the big buildings towering into the blue summer sky to the southwest. Had Mario "disappeared" in the hoodlum sense? It was more than likely.

⋅§

JOE WAS HAVING a very busy morning. It seemed to him it had only been a few minutes ago that he'd looked at the clock and noted that it was 9:15, but now another look and it was nearly 11:30. He'd been reviewing the reports on a certain important case that had taken thousands of man-hours and yet seemed to be getting no place fast, and the lieutenant had asked him for an analysis with recommendations. This was the type of police work Joe did best. He was always coming up with angles that had been overlooked and with good solid suggestions. He'd been moving from cubicle to cubicle, checking files and talking with people, and now it was nearly lunchtime and he felt no desire to let up.

A young police clerk finally located him as he was crossing a hallway and said: "Sergeant Ricordi, there's a girl wants to talk to you."

"Who is she? What does she want?" Joe obviously didn't wish to be bothered.

"She's sitting right down there," said the clerk; then he smiled. "I'll talk to her if you like."

Joe looked down the length of the hallway. At first he didn't recognize her in the kind of dress he'd never seen her in before—a modish dress, and she was wearing a little cloche hat. But it was Gina.

Joe handed the clerk a stack of papers, said, "Put those on my desk," then went out into the big anteroom to talk to Gina. He noted at once that she was getting admiring looks, and she deserved them, thought Joe; Gina was a very pretty girl and certainly at her best today.

Gina rose rather awkwardly, seeming embarrassed. "Well, I hope I'm not bothering you, Joe," she said.

"No," said Joe. "Something wrong, Gina?"

"No," said Gina. "I just dropped by to say good-bye."

"You're going someplace?"

"I'm going to Paris," said Gina. "Like I said I was."

Joe was really surprised. "What does Johnny have to say about that?"

"Oh, he doesn't care," said Gina. "I haven't even seen him for two days. Johnny's been drinking. Half the time he doesn't even come home. Now I don't know where he is. If you see him just say good-bye for me, okay?"

"Sure," said Joe. He felt awkward. What could he say? And then all the staring eyes made him uncomfortable.

"My baggage is already checked," said Gina. "I'm leaving for New York this evening. And my boat sails on Tuesday. I didn't know how to go about it, you know, but I talked to a fellow in a store and he sent me over to this travel agent, and it's just so simple, you wouldn't believe it."

Joe noted that Gina was on her best behavior, seeming much more ladylike than usual. Maybe it was best for her to get away. Johnny was not a bad guy in a sense, but really a no-good after all, crazy, disorganized, always in trouble, sometimes dangerous trouble. Johnny had done Gina one huge favor, no doubt about it. But Gina, in Joe's opinion, had more than paid him back, just with her company.

"Well," said Joe, awkwardly, "drop me a line from Paris."

"Will you answer me?"

"Yes, of course," said Joe.

"I'd like to have one friend to write me from home," said Gina, looking embarrassed.

"Well, sure," said Joe. "Be glad to."

They shook hands.

In the background one guy was saying in a low voice: "You better be careful what you say, Murphy.

She may be one of Ricordi's relatives."

"Varoom, varoom," said Murphy.

Gina gave with the Mona Lisa smile; then she turned and started away, gesturing good-bye over her shoulder.

The young clerk approached Joe and said: "The reports are on your desk, Sergeant," hoping that Joe would talk and that he'd learn something about that cute and pretty little Italian girl.

But Joe merely said, "Thanks," and returned to his office.

"Get Murphy out of here," cried one of the clerks. "He's in bad order."

"Varoom, varoom," said Murphy.

⌒

FOLLOWING The Man's instructions, Bones bypassed the big parking lot at the side of The Tangerine, which was nearly full of cars, drove down a wide alleyway beyond the restaurant proper, and finally found a small, private parking lot, fenced in but with an open gate. A low building, like a motel complex, projected back from the restaurant in a kind of L, and within the L was the private parking lot nearly full of cars. Beyond, the big restaurant was all lit up, crowded and noisy, with a jazz band going and a high tenor singing.

Bones found a parking slot, then got out and crossed to a door he saw in the motel complex marked Office. Bones kept looking about him. Quite a layout—and selling booze no doubt and running wide open. The Man was really an operator; a guy could coin money with this restaurant, but to The Man it was merely a front for an operation that made this one look like the poorhouse.

Bones entered the office, then stood looking about him. Beyond a railing was a switchboard with a black-haired middle-aged woman in attendance. On a big leather sofa in the front sat two well-dressed young men who, in spite of their fine clothes, were obviously hoodlums; one even had a slightly cauliflowered ear that had apparently undergone not very successful repairs. The whole place looked spanking clean and new and had obviously been done over at considerable cost.

"Mr. Macready?" asked one of the hoods politely.

Bones nodded.

"Just step in here," said the hood. "Mr. Degnan will be with you in a moment."

Bones wanted to laugh but refrained as he was ushered into a well-appointed officelike room, newly decorated but still retaining a certain aura of motel. Bones was left alone. He sat down, lit a cigar, and tried to compose himself. He felt strange, disoriented. Where was Mario? Where were Willie, Steve, Zell, and Fatso? But he was forced to admit that the latter quartet would look more than a little out of place with the dressed-up hoods and the strange aura of formal office that Degnan, or somebody, had managed to inject into the motel complex, which no doubt had formerly been merely a pleasure adjunct to the restaurant, either with whores in attendance or offering a convenient spot for assignations or quickies for the patrons, or both.

Was he the only one left? Bones began to feel definitely uneasy, but in a moment a familiar face was staring at him from the doorway. Kemper!

"Hello, Mr. Macready," he said, smiling and looking a little strange without his eyeshade. "When you get through with Mr. Degnan, come see my new office. Four doors down. Okay? Isn't this great? I've got two helpers now. We're expanding, you know. We've already added four new houses, with more to come. My work load will be unbelievable."

To Kemper it was just a work load, what else? It wasn't whores and hoods and trouble and misery, it was a work load.

"We've got an entirely new system," Kemper explained. "Everything is done here. All collections come here to be redistributed. It's a kind of financial center, right?" Kemper laughed again. He seemed to be a very happy man.

"It must have taken quite awhile to set this all up," said Bones, probing.

"Yes, it did," said Kemper, then hurriedly: "I've got work to do, you know. Don't forget to drop in and see me before you leave."

He ducked out. Bones laughed sardonically to himself. He felt very stupid. Behind their backs, The Man had brought about a completely new system, a new regime. None of what had happened seemed to have mattered at all. Ted and his crew and Mario had been doomed all along. And strangely enough, apparently Kemper had been on the inside from the beginning. Only Bones—who had obviously been given the old runaround—remained. It was both funny and disgusting.

The door opened and Maury Degnan propelled himself in, followed by a young man nearly a head taller than himself. Degnan was stocky, broad-shouldered, blue-eyed, and with a granite jaw. In the past he'd been an *enfante terrible* on the North Side, a young Irishman that the dagos simply couldn't conquer. Now, apparently, he'd joined up with the dagos.

The young man, dressed up like the hoods in the hallway, had a deceptively pleasant smile. His name was Corcoran, and he was known city-wide as Corky, a very tough boy.

Degnan shook hands in a perfunctory manner with Bones, saying: "Heard a lot about you. Never had the pleasure before," then he said: "I brought Corky in to shake hands. You can always get him here if you've got any questions or need anything. All right?"

Bones shook hands with Corky, whose hand seemed as big as a ham. There was a noticeable puffiness on the left side of Corky's face and what seemed to be the remains of a black eye, Bones noted. Corky smiled again, gave a kind of gung-ho gesture, and left.

Degnan got behind his desk and said: "Sit down, Mr. Macready. Make yourself comfortable. Had a long talk with The Man about you tonight. He thinks you're a pretty smart character." Degnan laughed bluntly, as if he'd made a joke. "Well . . . what do you think of the layout?"

"Fantastic," said Bones.

"I dreamed it up," said Degnan, "and went to The Man with it. He bought it. So . . . that's the story."

He sat staring at Bones as if that concluded the interview. But they talked on for nearly half an hour, going over the legal aspects of the business, the handling of arrests if any, the distribution of the funds, and the touchy matter of disbursement to Alderman Hruba, Captain Krumpacker, and some of the other police officials.

"It used to be handled all wrong," said Degnan.

"Handouts to the cops by individual houses—beat guys on the take. It was a mess. Now we turn it over to the big shots and let them handle it. Right?"

"Right," said Bones.

They talked a little while longer, then Bones rose to go. He had the definite feeling that he was gradually being worked out and was retained only because of his rapprochement with Krumpacker. Once they were certain they could handle that angle by themselves, Bones, the last of the old order, would be out, maybe pensioned. In fact perhaps he was already on a pension. Even the hoods were aware that it would not be wise to handle a man of Bones's standing roughly. All the same Bones had a sinking feeling in the pit of his stomach.

He made no inquiries about Mario, Willie, or anybody: they were gone, God knows where, and with these guys it was well to let sleeping dogs lie.

Degnan shook hands again perfunctorily, and Bones left. In the hallway the hoods smiled at him and pointed out Kemper's office, toward the end of the building. Kemper was at work with a big ledger in front of him, green eyeshade and all.

Rising, he proudly showed Bones about the place, pointing out the new adding machines, the new duplicators, the new typewriters—all, all brand new, a small fortune in equipment. Then he proudly displayed the safe to Bones. It took up part of one wall and looked as impregnable as Fort Knox. Some new operation, no doubt about it! The Man had poured the money in.

Bones walked thoughtfully to his car. This was either the end of something or a beginning. Who could tell? Things were not exactly as they had been; a new wind was starting to stir. Even The Man was beginning to have income-tax inquiries. Authority, federal authority, was slowly beginning to move in. In the city itself, in spite of protection and indifference on some sides, the hoods had built up over the years a crop of enemies who might possibly, eventually act. From any rational standpoint the whole situation was intolerable.

"But very profitable," Bones told himself as he got into his car and started out.

All the windows were open in the brilliantly lighted restaurant, and hubbub, the clatter of plates, the clink of glasses, and music drifted out into the warm Chicago night. The tenor was singing:

> "I'll get by
> As long as I
> Have you. . . ."

An almost excruciatingly inappropriate romantic song in such a setting, thought Bones as he drove back toward the Gold Coast and toward a type of life far more suited to his wishes, his desires, and his taste but made possible only by the likes of Degnan and The Man. Would he get out? Or should the question be: Would he get out in time?

◦§

Joe was just finishing up his dishes when there was a tap at his door. Joe had changed, in some ways drastically: he was beginning really to enjoy living again— food, wine, music, the radio, and not just as stopgaps. The other night he'd even gotten out his accordion and played a tune or two: surprised at how well he still remembered some of the old tunes, like "Sorrento" and "O Marie." He was even considering taking the kids, all four of them, to the dunes, something he hadn't done in years. Life seemed to be opening out for him at long last.

At the door was an apologetic-looking Italian, about seventy years old. He seemed shaken at the necessity of confronting Sergeant Ricordi, and he didn't seem to know whether to smile or remain solemn. He couldn't even speak. He thrust a note at Joe.

The note read:

> Dear old buddy:
> I got beat up and I can't get
> out of bed. Could you come
> see me?
>> Dago Al

An address was appended.

The address gave Joe a slight jolt. It was hardly more than half a block from where Joe himself had been born—the Old Neighborhood, with Little Italy just beyond and the legendary Five Corners, bloody battleground of the early booze barons, within walking distance.

"Are you a friend of Giovanni's?" asked Joe, a little disturbed.

"I am Aldo Marconi's father," said the old man.

Joe racked his brain. Who was Aldo Marconi? Obviously he was supposed to know. Suddenly it came to him. Young Aldo had made a brief reputation racing cars on local dirt tracks, and then had been killed in a terrible race accident. But . . . hadn't that been nearly twenty years ago?

"Oh, yes, Mr. Marconi," said Joe.

"Aldo and Giovanni were friends. I got old Doctor Rienzi to look after Giovanni. The doctor is eighty years old and retired, but he came and looked after Giovanni."

"Is he badly hurt?"

Mr. Marconi nodded. "Very badly, it seemed at first. But you know Giovanni. He is very brave and strong. He will be all right."

So Joe put on his coat and hat and with Mr. Marconi walked back to the Old Neighborhood, which was a mile or so distant, maybe further, at first through unfamiliar streets. Then suddenly Joe was walking back into his own past and it seemed very little changed: the same sights, sounds, and noises. The same narrow streets and alleyways, the same dim streetlights; even the same little storeroomlike picture shows, where he and the other youths had paid a dime admission to look at silent films—Charlie Chaplin, John Bunny, Flora Finch, and Max Linder. . . . Joe felt a strange kind of tightening in his chest. It was all very familiar and depressing and utterly remote from him now.

It was a warm night, and many were sitting out on the steps and even on the curbs. No special attention —the kind of attention that would have been paid to an obvious interloper—was paid to Joe. Joe's face fit right into the Old Neighborhood. He was apparently one of them.

"I haven't been back here for nearly twenty years," said Joe. "It looks the same."

"But it is not the same," said Mr. Marconi. "The young men are not the same. They are worse."

Joe made no comment, but in his memory they were bad enough in his time, many of them getting into serious trouble.

"It's the money," said Mr. Marconi. "All greedy. Never satisfied. They read the magazines and they want to be like that. The Church has no control over them anymore."

Mr. Marconi fell silent, and finally they turned down a side street and Mr. Marconi led Joe back between two buildings to a small ramshackle frame house at the rear.

"Giovanni's inside," he said. "I promised Giovanni I would bring you here. Now I have."

Joe tried to shake hands with Mr. Marconi, but the old man didn't note the hand in the darkness and without another word he wandered back up the narrow passageway.

Joe found the door unlocked and went in. An oil lamp was burning on a side table, and Giovanni was lying on an old couch just beyond. Near him was a fat Italian woman, who noted Joe's arrival and said: "I'll be going now, Giovanni. Then I'll come back."

In a muffled voice Johnny said: "Joe, this is my sister, Teresa."

Teresa was very awkward with Joe and didn't seem to know how to act. He tried to shake hands with her also, but by that time she had decided to leave and turned away.

At the door she said: "Don't worry, Giovanni. As soon as Mr. Ricordi leaves, I'll be back."

Joe walked over to the couch and stood looking down at Johnny—and he was a sight to see. His nose had been broken and was now crisscrossed with court plaster. His left eye was swollen shut and he could barely see out of the right, and his face, what you could see of it, looked lumpy and swollen. His right hand was in a cast, his left hand bandaged.

Joe said nothing; he merely shook his head.

Johnny tried to laugh, but he'd had some teeth knocked out, his lips were swollen, and it was painful. "Four of the bastards, Joe. And two went away carrying the other two. They never broke nothing but my nose and that was with a kick when I was laying on the pavement. I beat the hell out of them Irish bastards, Joe—only four was too many."

"What happened?" asked Joe.

"It was over Gina," said Johnny. "Because I stole her and beat up a whorehouse hood. Christ, the micks must've took over. It was Corky. He's bigger than me just by himself, and here he jumps me with three other guys. Where's Gina? Is she okay?"

Joe hesitated. "Yes, I think so."

"Did she leave yet?"

"Yes," said Joe. "She is on her way to Paris."

There was a long silence; then Johnny said: "She's some kid, Gina. But I never lived with no broad before and I couldn't stand it, like being married. I've always been in and out: bim-bam thank you ma'am. Not sitting around talking and cooking and all that. It bored me, so I got to drinking. See what I mean? But Gina's all right. She's some fine kid. She's old Brazzi the tailor's granddaughter. Did I tell you?"

"Yes," said Joe. "And don't talk so much. The thing for you to do is just lie there quiet."

Johnny tried to laugh again but it wasn't very successful. Finally he said: "The people here are just great, all of 'em looking after me. There I was laying in an alley all banged up, and then I woke up and I had noplace to go. I couldn't go back to the Bristol Arms looking like this, for Christ's sake. So I come here—and, hell, they practically turned out the guard. Old Marconi, who hates my guts, even tried to help. Me and Aldo used to be pals, but the old man didn't like me hanging around. One day he hit me with a big watermelon—it was when he had the fruit stand—and it busted and went to hell all over everything. He even got old Doc Rienzi for me . . ." Johnny broke off, groaned, and tried to shift into a more comfortable position.

"You need any money, Johnny?" asked Joe.

"You think I got you over here to put the bite on you?" cried Johnny resentfully. "I don't need no money. I got plenty. No; I just wanted to talk to you —and find out about Gina . . . and let you know something: Joe, they beat up the wrong dago. They got a bad dago after them. . . ."

"All right, Johnny."

Johnny groaned and lay back. It was no use. He couldn't get his meaning across without spilling his guts, as the guys said. And if ever—that could wait.

Joe could see that Johnny was feeling very weak but was still trying to put on an act. "All right," said Joe, "we've talked; now you get some rest. You were always wearing yourself out talking . . ."

"Or wearing *you* out," said Johnny, still trying to laugh.

Johnny seemed to be getting drowsy. Joe stayed for a little while longer; then when Johnny's head turned to one side and he fell into a doze, Joe went out very quietly.

Teresa was sitting on a tipped-back chair in the passageway, waiting. She got up at once when Joe appeared and said: "We thank you for coming here, Mr. Ricordi."

Joe nodded and said: "I think he's going to be all right."

"Yes," she said, "if he'd only be quiet. The doctor

gives him pills; he goes right on talking."

"Good night, Teresa," said Joe.

"Good night, Mr. Ricordi."

The "mister" made Joe uncomfortable but there was nothing he could do about it. Yet it put a distance between himself and Teresa and old Mr. Marconi. Marconi was a patriarch, so the "mister" was suitable. But nobody called reasonably young men mister in the Old Neighborhood. It just meant that in their minds, Joe was no longer one of them. And as a matter of hard fact, they were right.

•§

TIME PASSED. The newspapers were pursuing new sensations. The killing of Ted Beck by special deputies Fiore and Maxon was forgotten, a dead issue as new burning issues arose and burned themselves out one by one. Life went on as before, at the Northwest Precinct as elsewhere.

Joe was overwhelmed with work, as usual, but he didn't mind at all. Things had changed for Joe. He was less tense, less unapproachable, and according to Paula he had become almost human, which handed Dom quite a laugh. One night at Dom's, Joe had astonished them all by picking up Dom's accordion and playing half a dozen tunes. Dom hadn't touched the instrument in years, and sat staring. The Ricordis, in the old days, had been a musical family, and nearly all of them could play one instrument or another, though the accordion was favored.

The kids couldn't get over it. They always felt a little intimidated by Joe and his grim face. Now they didn't know what to think. And they almost had hysterics when Dom got up and began to dance in a style utterly unknown to them, and in a moment Paula joined him. The kids rolled on the floor, laughing.

It was quite an evening, and after the kids had gone reluctantly to bed, Joe, Dom, and Paula sat down at the table, sipped their wine, and had a long, pleasant talk. Without mentioning Johnny's name or the circumstances, Joe explained that he'd had to go into the Old Neighborhood, and then rather haltingly he gave Dom and Paula his impressions of what it had seemed like.

"I haven't been back in fifteen years, maybe longer," said Paula. "Not since my great aunt died."

"For me it's been longer," said Dom. "The only one left there was Uncle Luigi. After he died, I never went back."

All the younger Ricordis, luckier and maybe more industrious than the others, had moved away. Joe and Dom's two sisters were married and had left town. One was in South Bend, Indiana, the other in Lansing, Michigan; and Joe and Dom's three older brothers all lived in Chicago Heights and together ran a big garage and repair shop and a small trucking firm. Often Joe or Dom would see a truck moving down a Chicago street bearing the legend Ricordi Brothers, and it always made them feel proud. The Ricordis were now all as separated from the Old Neighborhood as the rest of the Chicago population.

"Why the old people stay there, I know," said Paula. "Why the others do, I don't know."

"It looks just the same, only smaller," said Joe. "Same movie theaters, even. I felt like I was seventeen years old."

All three sat in silent thought for a long time. They

almost never remembered the Old Neighborhood. It was as if it had never existed.

❦

JOE WAS PATIENTLY trying to explain what was to him a routine matter to a rather befuddled rookie when it happened. It was a hot August day, and all the doors and windows were open. First Joe heard the sound of what seemed to be hurried footsteps, scurrying. Then loud-voiced commands. People began to appear in the corridors.

"Go see what's wrong," Joe said to the rookie, who leaped at the chance of getting out from under the steady, disturbing eyes of Sergeant Ricordi.

In a moment the rookie hurried back. "It's the lieutenant," he said. "He collapsed. They're giving him oxygen, and the ambulance is on its way."

Joe hurried to Janowicz's office just in time to see him being borne out on a stretcher. His face was chalk-white, and he was hungrily inhaling oxygen from a carrier tank as two medics moved him carefully down a hallway.

In a moment an ambulance siren began to wail. Little by little the precinct quieted down, and the rookie wasn't able to escape after all. Joe renewed the interview and gave the rookie a long and detailed lecture on the correct way of making out reports and how important it was.

Finally, sweating, the rookie managed to escape.

Joe now took time out to eat his lunch. He had missed his usual time by nearly two hours, but work was work. He was very hungry and wolfed down his sausage sandwich in record time. He was just pouring out his second cup of coffee from the Thermos and thinking that tonight he would give himself a treat and take himself out to eat at Fuselli's, a good Italian restaurant on Sheridan Road where they cooked scampi very much to Joe's taste . . . when Sergeant Baker came into his office. Baker was in charge of police intelligence and was said to be very close to Captain Farrell. Joe almost never laid eyes on him.

"Thought I'd drop by rather than ring you up," said Baker. "It's important. The captain has a very busy schedule today, but he wants to see you. So stand by, Sergeant. I don't know when it will be. It might be late."

"I'll be here," said Joe; God knows he had plenty of work to catch up on.

Baker stood shaking his head. "I kept trying to tell Janny. But he wouldn't stop."

"Heard anything about him?" asked Joe, who was aware that among the top echelon Lieutenant Janowicz was "Janny." To the lower orders he was The Lieutenant, with all that implied, and to most it implied implacable authority.

"Well," said Baker, "he's still among the living. But this time he's got to take a long layoff—if nothing worse." Baker did not seem particularly sympathetic, Joe thought.

Nor was Joe, for that matter. He hardly knew Janowicz at all except officially.

The hours passed. The day people left, the night people came on. Finally at a quarter after eight Joe was summoned to the captain's office.

Several of the captain's cronies were lounging in the outer office, and there was still a lineup of those who hoped to see the captain before he left for the day, including members of the press.

But Joe was shown in at once. The captain's office

was large, old-fashioned, and ornate, its walls lined with pictures of the captain tête-à-tête with various worthies, from Mayor Big Bill Thompson to President Hoover, and from Jack Dempsey to Hank Wilson, and from Doug Fairbanks to Adolph Zukor, the movie producer. The captain was great for having his picture taken with celebrities. And then there were the plaques, commemorating one solemn occasion or another, and the walls were so crowded now that Joe noted that some of the plaques were stacked along the walls on the floor.

Captain Farrell was an old man, some said seventy. Most said he should have retired long ago. But he still had a thick head of hair, white and curly, and there were still remnants of toughness in his wrinkled, rather puffy face—the toughness that had taken him to the captaincy. For years the rumor was that he would be chief, but for some reason he'd always been passed over, and it was said he was embittered by this.

Joe stood at attention in front of his desk while the captain looked him over.

"Sergeant," said the captain, "I've got your record here right in front of me. And I don't see how it could be better. Certain matters beyond your control have prejudiced some against you, but I'm not going into that. These matters do not prejudice me. Tomorrow you move into the lieutenant's office. You'll be acting lieutenant until your promotion comes through, which will take a little time, as you know. Sergeant Ricordi, you are now my lieutenant, and I expect a lot of you—and I know I'll get it."

"Yes, sir," said Joe, almost unable to bring it out. He felt great elation and also something that might be called fear. Could he handle it? Was he adequate? His hands began to sweat.

The captain rose and shook hands with Joe and nodded and smiled, and that was that. Joe was now acting precinct lieutenant, a position of definite power. The captain went on to other things, buzzing the outer office.

Some way Joe got out and through the crowded waiting room and back into his own office. He felt like jumping up and down and yelling. Unable to contain himself, he immediately called Dom and Paula and gave them the good news. They began to laugh and yell and carry on, and in a moment he heard Dom say, "Paula, stop that," then, to Joe: "Believe it or not, Lieutenant, she's crying."

So Joe had his fine dinner at Fuselli's after all; almost a new man.

◆§

BONES WAS TRYING to make the most of his changed status, though he felt at times that he was moving in a kind of limbo. Aside from his small practice, he had nothing whatever to do, though the checks still came rolling in. So why should he complain? Yet on the other hand, how long could it last? You don't make money like this for no reason at all. Besides, it was bad for his ego, and Bones, being highly intelligent, was aware of that. A hoodlum, a tough Irish hoodlum, had worked him out.

At first he'd occasionally called Degnan and they would talk briefly, with Degnan obviously anxious to break off the conversation. The last time Bones called and found Degnan out, Degnan hadn't returned the call. To add to Bones's feeling of frustration, The Man had gone to Florida, where he had a palatial home; in fact he had a whole island just off the coast. Why had

The Man gone to Florida in the summer? And why hadn't The Man called Bones before leaving, or at least dropped him a line?

To add to Bones's growing dissatisfaction, he now had a rival for the company of Daphne, whom Bones had been taking for granted for some time now. The rival's name was Leland Graf; he was about fifty, a widower, and a junior partner at Beggs Inc. "I always seem to be haunted by Beggs Inc.," Bones observed to himself sourly.

Many men wanted to take Daphne out and be seen with her. It was well known that she was one of the richest women in Chicago. Some were obviously planning how to get part of that money—including Bones, in a rather lackadaisical way; others merely wanted the publicity of her presence; a few no doubt dreamed of marrying her. But there was little you could say in a derogatory sense about Leland Graf; he was eminently respectable—and rich. He wasn't hoodlum-rich, like Bones, but was backed by good solid wealth, and he would continue to get richer, especially if it was true that the market had nowhere to go but up. The brokerage business was booming, Beggs Inc. led the pack, and Graf was a partner.

Bones figured he was in trouble in regard to Daphne, and this brought about another disturbance of the ego. And Bones found himself becoming irritable and hard to get along with; very unusual with him, as his whole life had been predicated on the ability to get along with others, come rain or shine—in fact to take advantage of his equanimity, his lack of emotion, his superior imperturbability in comparison with others.

Let's say Bones was not a very happy man at the moment, especially tonight, as the uses of this world seemed so stale, flat, and unprofitable (as they had to Mario during his record hangover) that he'd decided to have his dinner served in his apartment while he listened to radio or otherwise hilariously regaled himself. He was tired of reading; he'd read too much already. Transient women were expensive and a problem—and what was left? The theater? Movies? He shuddered at the thought. Opera? As far as he was concerned, opera was a social event, like a charity ball, and had little or no entertainment value—not for him, certainly.

In fact Bones was succeeding in talking himself into a state of mind that bordered on melancholia. A healthy man takes pleasure in life, life in its simplest forms. At the moment Bones took pleasure in nothing, nor could he think of anything that might divert him or change his mood. Nor did he look forward to his dinner, no matter how elegant or exotic. And he suddenly remembered a line: "Black melancholy is the enemy of man." Where had he read it? In Burton? He couldn't remember. But it no doubt dated back to college days at the University of Michigan. To him, then, it must have seemed like a gag line. What did he know about melancholy then?

The phone rang and a robust voice came on. "William? Ben. We just came in off the lake. We hit a squall and almost upset, and I'd like to get quietly drunk and so would Irma. Had dinner yet?"

"Well, I . . ." said Bones hesitantly. The Moselys, though well-meaning people, bored him. And he was hardly in a mood for . . .

"William," came Daphne's voice, "come and have dinner with us. We were almost drowned. Don't you want to hear all about it?"

He definitely did, and he joined them in the dining

room of the hotel much sooner than they had expected. They were in yachting clothes, Mosely looking like a sea captain in his dark-blue sea coat with the
buttons and the braid. The ladies were in white. It was
a pleasure to see them, a definite pleasure, and black
melancholy began to recede.

"Leland will be joining us in a little while," said
Daphne, "and we'll have to tell it all over again, but
anyway . . ."

Black melancholy returned, and William tried hard
to hide his exasperation as Mosely took up the tale of
their almost-drowning as if it were a sea epic like *Moby
Dick*. Bones felt again that he'd been trapped. In fact,
it seemed to him that he was getting trapped quite a
lot lately. And feeling stupid merely added to his present woes of the spirit.

❧

DAVE SANTORELLI at home in the bosom of his family
was himself struggling with a state of mind. The teens
were at camp and that was worrisome in itself; much
could happen to kids at camps. The baby was crying
a lot, and Frances, his wife, had botched up the dinner
—not that he blamed her for that. She'd had a very
trying day, not only with the baby, but with a
stopped-up sink, entailing the expense of a plumber.

Now the uproar was over for the day. The baby
slept. And Dave and his wife were having a quiet cup
of coffee together. This had become a nightly ritual,
after the dishes had been washed and dried, the
kitchen put in order, and the table set for Dave's early
breakfast. A long silence.

Finally Frances said: "I'm sorry everything went

wrong tonight, Dave. I know you look forward to dinner."

Dave groaned slightly. "I don't see how you do it day after day," he said.

Frances studied him for a moment, then said: "And I don't see how *you* do it day after day, Dave. That's a terrible job."

"And I'm not even very good at it," said Dave.

Frances stared at her husband in surprise. She'd never heard him say a thing like that before. "What are you talking about?"

"Well, I'm forty and a median-grade detective," said Dave. "Joe Ricordi is forty and he's now lieutenant at Northwest . . . so it must be that I'm not very good at it."

"Oh, that's silly, Dave," said his wife. "Drink your coffee."

So Dave drank his coffee and tried to put a brave face on the matter; all the same he felt definitely discouraged about his prospects. In fact, though he'd been praised by Sluggo for his work on the Maria Ricordi case—for definitely identifying the suspect—in his secret heart he knew he wouldn't have come close if it hadn't been for the help of Joe Ricordi. What he didn't know was that without Johnny Albert, nobody would have come close . . . and that Joe had had as little to do with it as Dave himself.

"Francie," said Dave, "you haven't got much of a husband."

His wife came over to him, patted his head, kissed him on the cheek, and said: "You are all the husband I want."

Which brought Dave a little solace, because he was sure she meant it; he began to enjoy his coffee.

GOOD-BYE, CHICAGO

§

IT WAS September now and Acting Lieutenant Joseph Ricordi, known behind his back at the station as Tough Joe, as at Downtown Maheny was known as Sluggo, received a letter from Gina, which read as follows:

Dear Sergeant Ricordi:

I promised to write you but I got so busy I just didn't do it. We are going to stay here for a while, it might be till winter. Lud is trying to sublease his apartment in Chicago. You wouldn't believe Paris. Lud says there are more Americans here than French. He calls them x-patriots. I guess that means they like France better now.

Everybody gets drunk, the Americans, I mean, not the French, even in the daytime. But Lud hardly touches a drop as I had enough of that problem with Johnny. I don't know where to write him so say hello for me, please.

I'm having a lot of trouble with a Spanish painter who is a silly fool but Lud says he's a great artist. He wanted to paint me—so he did. So he kept wanting to paint me so he bored the life out of me so Lud had to throw him out of the flat. And he got drunk and the john-darms arrested him right outside our building. These guys are crazy, a lot of them. I'm glad Lud's so sensible.

How's Chicago? I'll bet it's hot right now. Paris is hot too but not like Chi. Oh, I'm having a fine time. I'm so glad I came. I tried to model clothes but I'm too short. Lud's exhibition at this little gallery was quite a success and he sold two pictures. He painted a fine one of me like the one in the Louvre and the Spanish guy, Lucas, saw it and got all stirred up so he wanted to paint me too. He's a nut. He kept trying to get me to run away to Spain with him. You think Johnny's weird? You should meet these people.

Well, I've run out of paper. So I will close with all best wishes.

Gina

All this in a rounded, rambling, childish hand that Joe had to puzzle over to read. What would ever become of Gina? No matter. It would be better than what she'd been through.

Having little time for such things, Joe tried to locate Johnny so he could read Gina's letter, but apparently Johnny had disappeared from the scene, and Joe, preoccupied with his work load, which seemed to grow heavier day by day, soon forgot all about Johnny.

◅§

THE WEEKS PASSED—it was October now—and one night when Joe got home from work, he heard the phone ringing inside his apartment. Certain it was the station calling—another emergency?—he hurried in to answer it. It was Johnny, and Joe had to reorient his thinking. Johnny? It was almost as it had been when Johnny had suddenly emerged from the past, with the help of Gina.

"Hi, Lieutenant," cried Johnny. "Long time no see."

"Where the hell have you been?"

"First I had to get well, right? And now I'm fit as

a fiddle but don't try to pluck my strings." Johnny roared with laughter. "I heard a broad say that the other night and it broke me up. Well . . . otherwise I may have a few guys looking for me, and I've been holing up. Right back in the old place. Know where I mean? So . . . Lieutenant . . . they hit this dago once too often, and I'm ready to turn fink and make a captain of you. Right? So get over here . . . if you're interested. And no money involved."

Joe thought it over. Johnny was obviously back in the Old Neighborhood, a reasonably short walk away, but Joe was tired and hungry, and besides he was dubious of Johnny's intentions. It didn't sound like Johnny. Something was up.

"Hey, are you still there?" cried Johnny. "This is the best offer you've had today, that's for sure."

Joe still hesitated. After all, he was no longer Sergeant Ricordi, he was Acting Lieutenant Ricordi and virtually in charge of the station, and Johnny was now an even more dangerous companion than before.

"You want to write me about it?" asked Joe.

There was a blank, then Joe heard Johnny swearing. "My Christ," cried Johnny, "have you got the swellhead already? Maybe I better come in and fill out a questionnaire. Are you kidding? This is big, Joe, big. . . ."

Joe finally made up his mind to take one more chance on Johnny and then make an end of it. "All right," he said. "I want to shower and change my clothes and eat dinner. I'll be there as soon as I can get there."

"Okay, old pal," cried Johnny. "You won't be sorry. Take your time. Teresa's whipping me up a good dago dinner. Great old girl, Teresa. I'm going to see if I can't get her married again; no good being a widow.

It's like being a nun; you just don't get none. . . ."
Johnny laughed loudly, then hung up.

Joe stood, shaking his head. Only one Johnny.

So HERE WAS Joe back once more in the Old Neighborhood, an acting lieutenant of the Chicago police. He'd brought off a long shot, no doubt about it; partly by luck, partly by hard work, but mostly by subduing his nature to the demands of his duties. The Maria affair had thrown him almost completely off the track. He had nearly committed himself to foolhardy acts at the expense not only of himself but of his children. Thinking back on it, he wondered now how he had ever been able to get through that desert of three empty years, then through the even worse nightmare that followed.

The weather had turned unseasonably warm. Doors and windows were wide open and people were sitting outside, on steps and curbs. Kids were playing in the street, running and hiding games, as Joe himself had played in these same streets. He heard the plinking of a mandolin, yet it was not an Italian tune but a pop song. The mandolin, the violin, and the accordion had been the instruments of the Ricordi family. . . .

Joe tried to shake off these involuntary incursions into the past. Unlike Johnny, it was not his normal way of thought, and for reasons unknown to him they depressed him.

He found Johnny sitting at a table with an oil lamp on it, with his chair tipped back, sipping wine from a water tumbler. Teresa was sitting nearby in the shadows, as if patiently attending to Johnny. She got up at once when Joe came in.

"Good evening, Mr. Ricordi," she said with a slight

inclination of her head. Teresa had never gotten out of the Old Neighborhood; though only forty-odd, she remained one of the Old People.

"It's lieutenant now, Teresa," said Johnny, who seemed to be amused by his sister.

"I know you want to talk," said Teresa. "I'll go next door till you're through."

She departed hurriedly. Johnny sat shaking his head over her.

"Hell," he said, "she might as well be back in that dago village where the Albertos came from. I can't even remember the name of the damned place. Well . . . Joe, sit down. Take a load off."

Joe sat across the table from Johnny and lit a cigarette. Johnny shoved the bottle in his direction.

"I heard from Gina," Joe said. "One letter. She didn't know where to write you."

Johnny rubbed a big hand across his face and considered. "I guess they're never coming back," he said finally. "I went over to the apartment one night, expecting them to be there. I still got a key. Nothing. So I went in. I was short of dough at the time. I felt like clouting some of them pictures of his and seeing if a fence would give me anything. Then I remembered Gina said they were just drawings and studies or some damned thing; that's why he left 'em around like that. Not worth much, or anything. So I came out clean. . . ."

Joe said nothing. He just sat studying Johnny's face. Johnny was always ribbing people, trying to get a rise out of them.

"Well," said Joe, finally, "you could have taken the doors off the hinges and lifted out the plumbing."

"Never thought of it," said Johnny, roaring. "What

do you know! Never changes, my old pal—even if he is brass, now. Did they give you a uniform with braid yet, for special occasions, like opening telephone booths and peanut stands?"

"Yes," said Joe. "I've got a dress uniform now. But I had to buy it. In fact I'm still paying for it."

"Boy, you ought to put it on and come down here in the daytime and show the Old People what a dago can do if he puts his mind to it."

Silence fell. They sipped their wine and smoked. And finally, at long last, Johnny came out with it—the whole Maury Degnan setup at The Tangerine. Joe sat in tense silence. Johnny even brought out a map and pointed out the location to Joe.

"Look," said Johnny. "I've been checking. And part of that property may be in the jurisdiction of the Northwest Precinct. It might be your baby, Lieutenant. Unless of course you don't mind whorehouses running wide open all over the place and whorehouse bouncers going around beating people up all over the city. Here's one for you: them four micks from The Tangerine beat me up in your precinct, Lieutenant . . . How do you like that one?"

"File a complaint," said Joe bluntly, "and I'll have them brought in."

"Do I have a witness? But to hell with that. What about this mess I'm handing you? It's yours—for free."

"It will have to be investigated," said Joe, realizing that this was a hot potato of frightening proportions, what with the grapevine flying around about Captain Krumpacker and the Southwest Precinct.

"So investigate it. Bust it wide open. Let's run them sonsabitches into the river, Joe. I told you they beat up the wrong dago, and I've really got the goods on them and their lousy operation. Right?"

Joe didn't stay much longer. He felt very disturbed and nervous. What a thing to have dumped in your lap, in the first months of your term as lieutenant of the precinct!

After he got home Joe sat, giving this extremely dangerous and unsettling business a lot of hard thought. Should he simply ignore the knowledge? Should he pretend to play along? Or should he face it squarely? But Joe was wasting time in thinking. His own character, his own instincts, would make the decision. And it was soon made. This was a matter beyond Joe's competence and power—it was a matter of overall police policy. It could not simply be ignored. Joe made up his mind that the next day he would take it up with Sergeant Baker, who would no doubt want to sound out the captain.

The decision made, Joe went to bed and slept soundly.

◦§

As in the case of Ted Beck's whereabouts, Joe had got a new map of the district and redrawn Johnny's wrinkled and smudged exhibit. Sergeant Baker sat studying it with intense concentration, a little pale, silent, as if slightly stunned. Joe had already given him all the information, and it was obvious at the moment that Baker was not sure what to do with it or about it.

"This is from a very reliable source?" he asked finally.

"Very. I'd count on it," said Joe. As far as Joe was concerned, Johnny had proven himself over and over.

"Of course," said Baker, "the demarcation business will have to be turned over to experts . . . the surveyors . . ."

"I think that's secondary," said Joe.

Baker sat on for quite awhile in silence. Good God, what an uproar this might cause! "Well," he said at last, "there is really nothing I can do about this. But as soon as the captain gets in, I'll take it up with him. The truth is he's got a very busy schedule today . . ."

Joe just sat looking at Baker, tough, menacing, without even knowing it or meaning to be.

". . . but this being such an important matter. . . ."

Baker left, talking as if to himself. One of Baker's main functions was weeding out the undesirables in the precinct or seeing that real malfeasance or prejudicial conduct was brought to trial. But this! It might damn a whole precinct; it wasn't just a matter of individuals. . . .

◆§

SEVERAL WEEKS passed, and it was almost November. Twice Johnny phoned and was told both times that the "matter was in the captain's hands." The third time Johnny called and was given the same reply, he yelled: "Well, I'm not going to wait much longer," and hung up before Joe could ask him what he meant. Joe was getting more than a little tired of Johnny and his vindictive one-man crusade against the "Irish whoremasters," as Johnny called them.

Finally, abruptly, one day Joe was called to the captain's office. Baker was present, sitting at the captain's right. The captain's curly white hair was rumpled, and he seemed vaguely disturbed, not his usual rather tough, inattentive self.

"Ricordi," he said, "you presented me with a prize package. How did you come by this information?"

Joe hesitated slightly, then said: "It was passed along to me by an informer."

"Was he paid?"

"No, sir. He did it as a favor."

The captain exchanged a glance with Baker. "Well . . . Lieutenant," said the captain, "I have taken this up with the highest authority, and believe me there was an uproar. And there is very little more that I can say about this. Under no circumstances are we to act in any way. And the whole thing is top secret among the three of us. Do we understand each other?"

"Yes, sir," said Joe.

"And Lieutenant," the captain went on, "I want to commend you for your diligence. But remember . . . this is top secret, and if anything leaks out from the Northwest Precinct, we are in very bad trouble. Not just you, not just Sergeant Baker, but me as well. Are we all clear?"

"Yes, sir," said Joe, and Baker nodded slowly and emphatically.

Later, in the outer corridor, Baker put his hand on Joe's shoulder and said: "I'll make one observation, then I'll never mention the subject again. You really struck a nerve. You don't know what the captain's been going through."

Nor did Joe want to know. He didn't want to hear any more about it. He felt badly discouraged. Was the grapevine right? Was there a top-echelon fix? If so, what could he do? He'd just have to live with it if he wanted to continue in the police department, which he most certainly did. It was one thing to have one suspect precinct, but all the precincts? Joe shuddered inwardly at the thought.

But could it be? Joe finally decided that it could not. Captain Farrell might have his weaknesses and his drawbacks, but a chiseler he was not . . . and nobody could ever make Joe believe that he was. The more Joe thought about the problem, the more mysterious it became, so finally he managed, sensibly, to throw it off and return to the stack of papers on his desk and to the running of the station. That was his job, the running of the station; long-range policy matters were the captain's business, and from now on Joe intended to stay out of them.

All the same he couldn't help feeling very uncomfortable about the whole thing. And what about Johnny? Wouldn't it be best after all just to forget about Johnny?

The only trouble was that Johnny didn't forget about him. He called a night or two later and insisted that Joe come and see him, either that or he would come and see "the lieutenant," as he put it. This made Joe sore, and he decided that he would go and see Johnny—and for the last time. This was a very bad association for him, and the time to break it off was now, face to face.

When he arrived, Johnny was alone. Johnny noted at once the expression on "Tough Joe's" face, and he did not as usual come up with any quips or stories. He had stepped out of line, and Joe had had enough. It was very plain.

"I've got something to tell you," said Joe, "and I didn't want to do it over the phone. I've had a bellyful of you, Johnny. I don't want to hear another word about this goddamned business. And don't pester me anymore. I won't stand for it."

"I put the best thing around in your lap . . ."

"Why?"

"Well, we're pals, ain't we?"

"Try again."

"All right, so I want them no-good sonsabitches taken care of. Don't you?"

"Never mind what I want—and don't give me anymore of that old-pal stuff if you think it gives you a license to keep calling me and pestering me and even threatening me . . . "

Johnny fell silent. Joe studied him for a long time, then turned and went out. In a moment Johnny came running after him up the passageway.

"All right, all right, Joe," he said. "Forget it. No more."

He tried to shake hands with Joe, but Joe was steamed, ignored the hand, and went on about his business.

Johnny just stood there looking after Joe, then turned and went back. Teresa was waiting.

"Lieutenant Ricordi didn't stay very long tonight," said Teresa.

"No," said Johnny, "he didn't."

Then he went inside, lay on the couch, and stared at the ceiling. Teresa finished up her household chores; then she went across the passageway to see if Mrs. Gregori's little daughter was okay for the night —she had the flu—and when she returned, she noted that Giovanni was still staring at the ceiling. Was he sick or what? This just wasn't like Giovanni at all.

Night. And Willie was eating the cheapest thing on the menu, a bowl of watery soup, at Duke's open-front diner, when someone gently touched his elbow. Willie shied off slightly as he turned. Then he stared. The creep, Sheffy! Willie had forgotten that he existed. Sheffy had his usual timid smile, as if apologizing for living.

"Well," he said, "I finally found you."

"You been looking for me?" asked Willie. "Why?"

"Don't you remember? You said if I ever had any more info, to come to you . . ."

So much had happened to Willie in so short a time that he drew a blank. What did the creep mean?

"And Steve hit me to make me remember," said Sheffy, laughing apologetically, putting his hand to his mouth like a kid.

Willie remembered. God, how long ago that seemed now, happenings in another world, a world of power and prosperity.

"Yeah, I remember," said Willie, all his instincts aroused. Was it good info? What was it worth? Could he make a strike? God knows he needed to.

"Have you had your dinner?" asked Sheffy.

"No," said Willie. "I just scoffed this bowl of soup to tide me over till dinner."

"I'm hungry," said Sheffy. "Let's go have dinner, and we can talk. I know a good place where nobody goes." Sheffy meant nobody in their world.

"Okay," said Willie with a joviality that surprised Sheffy. "But the dinner's on you."

"Sure, sure," said Sheffy, and he guided Willie to a

huge Ontra Cafeteria on the nearby boulevard.

The place made Willie uncomfortable. It was brilliantly lighted and with a shiny, functional air about it that was alien to Willie. As it was an odd hour, it was less than a third full and its large emptiness also disturbed Willie, who was used to small, crowded, ill-lit places. But when he saw the loads of food all laid out for inspection, his spirits rose and he grabbed up a tray with alacrity.

"I'm warning you," said Willie, "I got a hell of an appetite."

"Fine," said Sheffy, "me too." And shortly thereafter they appeared at a table with trays loaded to the rims and began to eat.

Sheffy was eating for pleasure and taking his time about it. But Willie had to restrain his wolfish instincts; he was really hungry. And as they ate, Sheffy slowly began to get a different picture of the Willie he'd known, the powerful Willie, the Willie he had carried in his mind. He noted Willie's ill-cared-for clothes; he noted the hungry eating, even though Willie was doing his best to take it slowly. Had he made a mistake in coming to Willie?

"What's this info, Sheffy?" asked Willie with a mouthful.

"It's very important, very touchy," said Sheffy. "And it's worth a lot of money."

"So . . . fine. Let's make us some money."

There was a long pause. Sheffy could not make up his mind what to do. This was very big, one of the biggest he'd ever had or was likely to have. He was terrified he'd blow it some way.

"What've you been doing lately, Willie?" asked Sheffy. "Aren't you with the organization anymore?"

"Of course I am," said Willie, "but I had the flu, then pneumonia and nearly died. I'm just getting back on my feet."

The true tale, of course, was much more dire. Willie and his men had been unceremoniously bounced as soon as Degnan and Corky took over—lucky for them it wasn't worse. And Willie hadn't saved his money. He'd had the feeling it would never end, like the papers said about the stock market, no place to go but up. He'd made a lot of money under Ted and he'd spent it on women, gambling, and booze. And when he was bounced by Degnan, his total bankroll had amounted to less than five hundred dollars. And he hadn't even been careful with that, feeling sure he'd catch on someplace.

And then his luck had run out entirely. In Chicago in 1928 there was a minor flu epidemic, similar to but not as severe as the disastrous one of 1918. Willie came down with it and finally wound up in a hospital ward with over fifty other flu patients. What a nightmare! And then it had gotten worse: pneumonia, and Willie came close to cashing them in.

And now here he was with a few carefully nursed dollars in his pocket and unable to get up his room rent, and a beef with his landlord coming up.

He studied Sheffy, who didn't make his precarious way by being a fool. He was sure that by now Sheffy had come pretty close to figuring out his status.

"So then you can get to Degnan?" asked Sheffy.

Willie paused, then said: "Sheffy, I'm going to level with you. Degnan got rid of all of Ted's old guys, including me. Then I got the flu and nearly died of pneumonia, and I've had it rough ever since. But I got an ace card . . ."

Sheffy felt better now. Willie had leveled. If he'd gone on trying to lie, Sheffy would have brushed him off one way or another. "You have? What is it?"

"I can do better than Degnan. I can get in touch with Bones, who is still in. He'll listen."

In fact Willie had gotten in touch with Bones not too long ago, and Bones had promised to try to help him, get him something to do; but Willie had heard no more.

"Okay," said Sheffy. "If you can set up a meeting, you're in, Willie. But he must bring the money."

"How much?"

"Twenty-five hundred dollars."

Willie whistled. "And what's my part?"

"Since the info is all mine," said Sheffy, "I'll give you five hundred."

Willie tried to hold out for seven hundred and fifty, but Sheffy, who realized that finally he had the upper hand over Willie, wouldn't budge. In the past there would have been the danger of big Steve beating it out of him and leaving him with nothing. But that danger was over. Willie was in trouble, in need; that was obvious. And Sheffy began to wonder if he hadn't been too generous.

Finally they settled on five hundred.

◆§

BUT IT WAS far from simple. Bones would not return Willie's calls, and Willie never managed to find him in —Willie still had his direct-line number. Meanwhile Sheffy had moved in with Willie and was paying the rent, which he intended to deduct from Willie's share. Willie began to get a little frantic.

But one night his luck changed. Bones answered the phone.

"Willie," said Bones, "I've got to insist you stop bothering me. I've asked around and nobody wants you, Willie. And I can't put you on a personal pension, now can I?"

"You got it wrong," said Willie. "I'm trying to do you a favor. Right now I'm teamed up with the guy who saved Ted's life, at least for a while. He tipped Ted off and Ted lammed. He's got info that's worth a lot of money. He says it's a matter of life or death." Then Willie told Bones what it would cost him.

If he'd caught Bones at another time, Bones would have laughed at him. But for quite awhile now Bones had felt a growing uneasiness. The Degnan operation was booming beyond all expectations, and it was not going unnoted, especially by outraged citizens of the district. It was too open, too brash, too brazen. In the old days under Mario and Ted, it had been a hit-or-miss operation not causing much comment; now it was more like an industry.

Bones was willing to listen.

"Fine," said Willie. "I'll put my partner on."

And so Sheffy talked with Bones, and a typical Sheffy-meeting was set up: a daytime rendezvous in the waiting room of the Pennsylvania Station in The Loop, a large, crowded place where it was very hard to trap anybody.

❧

BONES WAS a little late and came hurrying in, looking about him. Then he crossed quickly to the newsstand. Willie was there, reading a paper. With a motion of his eyes and head, he indicated Sheffy, who was looking through the magazines on the rack. Bones quickly got the idea, moved over beside Sheffy, and picked up a magazine.

"The money?" said Sheffy, not looking at him.

Bones hesitated, then passed it over. Sheffy examined it briefly, separating it with deft, practiced fingers, then, apparently reading a magazine, he said: "The Degnan operation is being investigated by undercover men working out of the chief of police's office, in cahoots with investigators for the grand jury and the crime commission."

Bones tried to ask a question, but Sheffy moved away quickly to the end of the rack and started to study another magazine.

Bones was so stunned it took him a moment to realize that no more questions were necessary. His hands shaking, he bought a paper at the main stand and hurried out. Willie was no place to be seen.

In a moment Willie appeared at the far end of the rack, and Sheffy slipped him his take. While Willie was surreptitiously examining it, Sheffy just seemed to melt into the crowd and noise of the big station, where redcaps were hustling baggage, trains were being called, and travelers were rushing in every direction in a kind of ballet of controlled confusion.

To Willie's surprise, Sheffy hadn't taken out the rent money after all: a clear five hundred clams—and Willie now had a new lease on life.

܀

BONES HAD ALWAYS been a man of quick decisions, in crisis or otherwise, and this was no exception. He immediately began making preparations to say good-bye to Chicago. He looked into the conditions of his office lease and decided to sublet; his hotel was no problem, as he had no lease there but merely paid a monthly bill. As for his assets, they consisted of cash, bonds, clothes, jewelry, and an expensive automobile —all movable. And as for friends?

"Who needs them?" thought Bones, and as a matter of fact it would give him great pleasure now to say good-bye to Daphne permanently. Daphne took him for granted, thought he was on the hook. Bones started laughing to himself, conjuring up the scene.

Good-bye, Daphne.

◆§

But after the initial shock, Bones had settled down emotionally, and he began to have second thoughts and to see the whole situation in better perspective. It wasn't just a simple matter of moving on, of moving back to Detroit and opening a law office there. It was impossible for him to act in a vacuum, as if he were just anybody. He was a special person, on more or less intimate terms with The Man. Let's say Sheffy's info was correct. Suddenly Bones disappears from the scene, and shortly thereafter arrests are made or subpoenas handed out. How would it look? Well, it would look so bad that Bones might have unwelcome visitors in Detroit. The Man was no respecter of person when it came to something big, like an apparent high-echelon sellout.

The Man was still in Florida and couldn't be reached, and Bones hated to call Degnan, who had openly (over the phone) shown his contempt for

Bones. But Bones had to swallow his pride and call Degnan; there was no other way.

As usual, Degnan was not available. It was Corky on the line trying to soft-soap Bones, as usual, so Bones said: "You tell Degnan this is the last time I'll ever call him, and if he doesn't return this call, he'll wish he had."

A minute later Degnan was on the line. "Macready," he yelled, "what the hell are you trying to do, threaten me? Now listen here—"

"You'd better listen," said Bones, "or you'll be sorry. . . ."

So Degnan listened, and Bones gave him the tale. Bones certainly expected a reaction, but not the one he got. Degnan burst out laughing. "Who you been talking to, them jerks down at the crime commission? That's a lot of slop. Nothing to it. Are you kidding?"

"All right," said Bones, "I'm on record as warning you. Remember? I warned you."

He hung up. In a few minutes Degnan called him back.

"Yes?" said Bones, very unfriendly.

"Where'd you get this slop, Macready?"

"From an underworld information peddler."

Degnan laughed and hung up.

But Degnan's reaction did not shake Bones, who had sensed an uneasiness in the atmosphere for a long time now. The Greeks had a word for Degnan's, and maybe even The Man's, attitude—*hubris:* pride goeth before a fall. And Bones made up his mind he would definitely not take the tumble with them. Things couldn't have been riper: The Man was in Florida on his island, and the big Southwest Side operation was in the hands of a hoodlum—a superhoodlum maybe, but just a hoodlum all the same—Maury Degnan.

Bones even began to feel good about the whole thing. He'd cleared his own skirts; now they could take it or leave it.

While he was showering before dinner, he made up his mind he would give a little dinner party in the hotel dining room, and then after a fine meal he'd announce his intentions to leave the city, or as his former friends would have said, blow the joint. He was anticipating the look on Daphne's face when the phone rang.

To his surprise it was Captain Krumpacker. "Macready," said the captain, "what is this nonsense you've been telling a certain party?"

"It's underworld information," said Bones. "I merely passed it along . . ." And then smiling to himself, he added: ". . . Out of a sense of duty."

"Why didn't you check with me? I assure you there is nothing to it. Don't give it a second thought."

"Well, I'm glad to hear that, Captain. Fine."

"We must get together one of these days."

"By all means," said Bones.

Even this didn't shake Bones's intentions. If not now, later. It was bound to come, and Bones intended to be off and away with all he'd won.

❧

BONES'S, or rather William's, little dinner party was quite a success: the Moselys, Daphne, Leland Graf, and Mrs. Wachtsheim, a rich widow who lived in the hotel and answered to the improbable name of Trixie. And William had arranged the menu himself: cold vichyssoise, lake perch with shrimp sauce, châteaubri-

and with châteaux potatoes, mixed French vegetables, crême brulée, and what passed for champagne in Chicago.

Daphne obviously made Trixie very uncomfortable. In spite of her fifty-plus years, Daphne was slim and chic, while Trixie seemed to be bursting through her clothes, though she dieted rigidly and even rode a stationary bicycle in the hotel gymnasium. And Daphne was still richer than Trixie, which made it even harder to bear.

William was enjoying himself immensely, especially as he noted the rather worshipful looks being cast on Daphne by Leland Graf. Well . . . after all, Bones thought, maybe they deserve each other.

By the time the Grand Marnier (or so the hotel called it) was reached, everybody seemed in a rather mellow mood, even Trixie, livened up and stirred into happiness by the champagne, her waistline forgotten for the moment, and her lesser millions.

Then William made his announcement. He was moving to Detroit to accept a very lucrative offer—or that was the way he told the tale—and in one week's time he would be on his way. This was his farewell party.

William noted the shock. The Moselys liked him, thought him fine company; Daphne had been taking him for granted, keeping him on the string; and Trixie was also beginning to have plans in regard to William Macready, who would really make her a very decorative partner; only Leland Graf was pleased but apparently the most surprised of the party.

"Well, William," said Daphne, "isn't this rather sudden?"

"Yes," said William. "But the offer was sudden."

The announcement had thrown a damper on the party, as William had hoped it would, and not long after the coffee things began to break up. The Moselys left first, pleading an early-morning rising, and finally Leland and Daphne made their adieux; William thought he noticed a rather reproachful look in Daphne's eyes, but maybe after all that was just wishful thinking on his part.

William and Trixie moved on to the bar, where there was music. Trixie refused further strong drink and settled for Vichy water. But William went on drinking, in fact he was rather drunk already, happily so, and he sat there tapping a foot while the trio played "Yes Sir, That's My Baby . . ."

◆§

Nobody was exactly sure how it had all happened. A dozen witnesses told a dozen different stories, which the police were painfully trying to collate and piece together. Apparently, on that cold late-November night, shortly after midnight, suddenly, out of a big vacant lot, just beyond The Tangerine, a group of men —estimated at from six to ten or more—appeared and advanced on the office complex. They were carrying shotguns and small automatic weapons and wearing dark hoods made from marine stocking caps with eye holes. Sudden gunfire from inside slowed them down temporarily but didn't stop them, and shortly they smashed their way in, wrecked the place, and apparently tried to blow the amazingly large safe. But far too much nitro or some other powerful explosive had been used, and instead of blowing the safe, they blew out one whole wall of the building, shattering it to such an extent that the roof at that end fell in. The fire that later gutted the office complex apparently was started by the explosion. While all this was going on —and being observed by many from the restaurant itself—"company security guards" arrived, and there was much promiscuous shooting, the guards operating from behind cars in the private parking lot.

But the fiasco of the safe brought about the end. The raiders fled into the darkness of the vacant lot and were not pursued.

It was a Chicago sensation, just the kind of happening the newspapers prayed for. Reporters swarmed all over the place shortly, and it was not long till extras hit the streets in all parts of town. The first extras, through haste, carried very sketchy accounts, mentioning casualties though not elaborating. But as a gray dawn fanned out over Lake Michigan, things were becoming clearer and more detailed accounts were being published; and the casualties were listed as follows:

> The dead:
> Giovanni Alberto, alias Johnny Albert, about 40
> Clement (?) Spinelli, about 40
> Marvin J. Kemper, bookkeepper for The Tangerine, 45
> Eugene "Corky" Corcoran, about 25
> The wounded:
> Grace Slavin, telephone operator, about 40
> Maurice Degnan, 35

Aside from this list, there were three unidentified dead and six unidentified (as yet) wounded.

The scare heads read: 7 DEAD 8 WOUNDED IN

W. R. BURNETT

WEST SIDE ROBBERY ATTEMPT.

And people could hardly believe their eyes. This sounded more like war than crime, and there was much viewing with alarm and what are we coming to . . . and the newspapers kept feeding the sensation all the next day and you could hardly hear anything else on the radio.

It was late in the morning before Bones heard the news. At first he couldn't believe it, and then he was afraid to believe it—possibly a whole multimillion-dollar operation wiped out, records gone, Kemper gone, hundreds of thousands of dollars destroyed, the papers stating that the contents of the safe were a total loss; Corky dead, Degnan wounded . . . and not only that—what a hell of a lot of explaining to do!

Bones felt very nervous and indecisive and poured down a couple of quick, stiff drinks that really bounced, as he'd had no breakfast as yet. Suddenly he felt drunk, and then for a moment fear took charge and he had, all at once, an almost overpowering desire to flee, to run away someplace, anyplace. But little by little he managed to calm himself. Nothing to do but to step up his departure a little bit, without making it obvious.

◆§

As FOR Joe, he was stunned. He'd known Johnny was wild, reckless, and crazy, but he'd had no idea he'd try to pull off a thousand-to-one-chance rip-and-tear assault like that, almost certain to fail. The bee in Johnny's bonnet had been much larger than Joe had imagined.

And the repercussions of this one event were endless. The chief of police and his investigators had now had their hands forced; impossible patiently to lie back now till they were sure of all their facts and had built up impregnable cases. The fat was in the fire: they had to act. Wholesale raids started in the Southwest Precinct, but they were not carried out by the police of that precinct, who were angered and bewildered by the turn of events.

One whorehouse after another was raided, and everybody inside was carted off to the tanks amid hysteria, violence, screaming, wild attempts to escape, scurrying bail bondsmen, frantic criminal lawyers, and scratched-up, injured but reasonably patient police. The paddy wagons were everywhere, their bells ringing through the night streets of Chicago, carrying a jam-packed, cursing cargo to one prepared outpost or another.

In twenty-four hours every whorehouse on the Southwest Side had been emptied of its contents and padlocked, and Captain Krumpacker and various other police officials, and even Alderman Hruba and Cyrus D. Travis III, of Ohio, had been handed subpoenas, though in the confusion of the forced-hand action, many managed to escape from Chicago. In fact there was a very large exodus. Krumpacker was removed as captain of the Southwest Precinct, and the chief sent in a whole new temporary staff.

POLICE SCANDAL ROCKS CITY, cried the yellowest tabloid.

The city was, of course, not "rocked." That was mere journalistic hyperbole. But some citizens, not knowing the facts, were shaken; yet most were indifferent, preoccupied with their own problems. To them it afforded momentary interest, a brief sensation almost immediately forgotten. Nevertheless, the newspapers did a land-office business in extras and tried their best to keep the ball rolling, sweating to provide a sensation a day; and, of course, all over the world, noting news from the USA, people were saying, "Chicago! Good God, what a town!"

◈

Joe did not think it was proper for him to attend the funeral of a big-time hoodlum like Johnny, but still he wanted to pay his respects. So he went at night to the Old Neighborhood and got in contact with Teresa, who seemed stunned, as if she couldn't believe such a thing had really happened to Giovanni, and so nervous and ill at ease in Joe's company that at first he was sorry he had come.

It was a cold November night, the streets empty, as Teresa led Joe to the Marinetti Funeral Parlor, where Giovanni was laid out in a fine large satin-padded coffin that had been provided, Teresa shyly explained, by old Mr. Marconi, who had taken up a collection among the small businessmen of the area. Giovanni had been known to all, and he had never harmed anybody in the Old Neighborhood; in fact, they were rather proud of him in their strange way.

Joe stood staring down at Johnny. He looked dead, but otherwise unchanged. Was there a heaven for the likes of Giovanni Alberto? Joe didn't know. He knew only what he had been taught. But hell had never seemed real to him, nor did it seem fair. It was a very rough and difficult world. Some men were lucky. Some were unlucky. Some lost the ball game completely by merely taking one wrong turn. But such thinking could hardly apply to Johnny. From the first he had gone his own way in spite of everything. So maybe it was true after all that for the persistent evil-doer there was a penalty that had to be paid. But Joe simply couldn't envision it.

He turned. Teresa, still-faced, was elaborately crossing herself and praying. He stepped outside, and in a moment she joined him.

"Teresa," he said, "if you get short of funds or anything like that, please call me."

"Oh, I'll be all right, Mr. Ricordi," said Teresa, then shyly, looking away from him, she added: "I may get married."

"Oh, that's fine," said Joe, wondering if Johnny had managed to promote a man for Teresa, as he'd promised.

They said good-bye, and Joe walked home through the cold, silent Chicago streets feeling a strong sense of relief as he passed beyond the boundaries of the Old Neighborhood.

◆§

THERE WAS A DIFFERENT atmosphere in the Northwest Precinct now. The issuance of the warrants had completely turned things around. During the worst of the uproar, things had sagged, morale-wise, in all the precincts, largely because of the bitter assaults on the CPD by the press and radio. Policemen were getting jeered at. There was a cartoon in a Chicago paper that showed a Chicago policeman begging a friend as follows: "Don't tell my mother I'm a Chicago policeman. She thinks I'm a racing tout."

But the CPD was cleaning its own house, and that

was becoming apparent even to a largely hostile press.

One afternoon Joe was called into the captain's office. He noted the usual anteroom full of petitioners and members of the press. But Sergeant Baker, one of the captain's true cronies, was waiting for him and immediately took him inside.

Captain Farrell's face looked red and healthy today, his curly white hair neatly combed. He even rose halfway and shook hands with Joe.

"Well, Ricordi," he said, "the confirmation came through. You are no longer acting; you are now my full-fledged lieutenant. Good luck. You may need it."

Joe was nearly speechless. Finally he said: "Thank you, Captain."

The captain nodded and smiled, and then he started buzzing, and Joe was on his way out, gently propelled by Sergeant Baker.

Joe felt wonderful. In fact he didn't know just how he felt. Ever since he'd been made acting lieutenant, there had been a small, nagging doubt at the back of his mind that he wouldn't be confirmed. Why not Sergeant Baker, as some had been asking around the station? He was well liked in spite of the controversial job he had, and he was known to be very close to the Old Man. But apparently the captain, a tough one himself, didn't consider Baker tough enough for the job, as Janowicz, who was now in the hospital on a semi-permanent basis, had proved not to be tough enough in the long run, though he had been the choice of the captain. Illness had been Janowicz's cross, bad luck that he could do nothing about it except struggle with it to the end.

The Christmas season was drawing near. Joe decided he'd take the whole family out to dinner on

Dom's day off, make a big thing of it, a holiday party —and not announce the good news till sometime during dinner. Where would they go? He finally chose Fuselli's on the near North Side, where the Italian food was excellent.

⋙

OUTSIDE the snow was falling rather heavily, but inside Fuselli's all was warm, comfortable, and pleasant. Around Fuselli's, Dom, as a table captain from Chancy's, was quite a big man (soon he would be a maître d', no?) and every effort was made to please the large Ricordi dinner party, including table decorations of sugar-candy snowmen and a wide assortment of Christmas candy for the kids.

Dom had bought Paula a fur coat, her first, and she was so proud of it that she refused to check it and had it draped across the back of her chair. The kids— Maria, Joe, Jr., Monica, and Sophia—were bright-eyed and full of hell and put away large quantities of antipasto, scampi, and veal, not to mention dessert. Three choices had been offered: biscuit tortoni, Neapolitan ice cream, or spumoni. Joe, Jr. decided on all three but his father quickly vetoed that, afraid that it might come to the stomach pump.

Wine was served to the adults. It was a very busy night at Fuselli's, but if anybody was neglected it wasn't those at the big Ricordi table in the corner.

"Well, Lieutenant," said Dom, a smile wreathing his wide, pleasant face, "here's to you." Dom and Joe looked nothing alike. It was hard to imagine they were brothers. Joe was a Ricordi, Dom a Vasari, a typical product of the mother's family. Joe was tough, Dom soft, but shrewd and able.

Paula and Dom drank to Joe, who tonight seemed much softer than usual, sort of humbly, even embarrassingly pleased with what was going on. Usually he seemed to Dom and Paula grim and far away and actually paying no attention to them or even to his surroundings. Had he finally become reconciled to life without Helga-Maria? It was a question they both wanted to ask but wouldn't think of asking. As a rule, Italians were outgoing, but Joe was not, never had been. Dom blurted out everything; Joe told you nothing.

The evening wore on. The food disappeared, and little by little the kids began to fall silent; they were full as ticks, tired—worn out by all the gaiety and noise—and beginning to get sleepy. Finally Monica put her head against her mother's shoulder and started to settle down.

"Oh, no, Miss," said Paula. "You sleep when you get home. No carrying out tonight."

And so the long dinner came slowly to an end. Dom got the pack ready to move, and Joe settled the bill, which startled him slightly, but well, hell, it was a special occasion, one of the few, and it was getting toward Christmas. Besides, he had had a large raise in pay.

The family was at the door waiting for Joe when a couple entered that immediately caught everybody's attention. The man was tall, slender, and conventionally dressed even to a big, modish camel's-hair topcoat, but his hair was long and he was bewhiskered and mustachioed. The girl was of medium size, even short, slim, with very close-cropped black hair, no hat, and wearing a wraparound fur coat that looked much too big for her.

The family stared at the couple, then started out,

shooed like chickens by Dom. Joe glanced at the couple, made a move to follow the family, then stopped stock still.

"Gina," said Joe.

"Joe," cried Gina.

She hesitated for a moment, then flung herself into Joe's arms. Joe was stunned. The family stared in amazement, the kids bug-eyed. How dare she get so familiar with the tough lieutenant?

Gina moved back abruptly with an embarrassed smile. "I was just so surprised to see you," she said. "Excuse me."

"She's a little effusive at times," said Everett, smiling; both had been doing considerable drinking and apparently were feeling no pain. "And it often leads to rather comical results."

Gina, with a certain amount of pride in her voice, introduced Joe to Ludlow Everett, and they shook hands.

"We just got back yesterday," Gina explained. "It's so cold. They're giving Lud a show in Laguna Beach, California, so I don't think we'll be here long. I hope not."

They talked on for a moment. No mention was made of Johnny. If she hadn't heard about what had happened to him, this was neither the time nor the place to bring it up. If she had heard, it was up to her to mention it.

Finally Joe indicated the family waiting for him, shook hands with Everett, smiled at Gina, and left.

The Ricordis moved toward their car in silence. Finally as they got in, Joe said to Dom, "Do you remember old Brazzi the tailor?"

"Of course I do," said Dom. "I used to deliver pants

for him. He'd give me a dime. He was always laughing."

"That's his granddaughter."

"Well, I'll be damned," said Dom, staggered.

And as they drove away, Paula said: "I remember the Brazzis. One of the girls was very, very pretty. That must be her mother."

"Yeah," said Dom, "the old guy would give me a dime and say, 'Now pleasa, boy, donta spend dat all in one-a place.' " Dom leaned back and laughed loudly. "So that's his granddaughter!"

"And here I thought they were swells," said Paula.

And so the Ricordi family drove homeward through the falling snow, and one by one the kids fell asleep.

Well, thought Joe, at least Giovanni did one thing he could be proud of, maybe two, if he'd managed to get Teresa a husband.

So maybe there were a few good marks in Giovanni's book of judgment after all.

⋅❧⋅

WILLIAM ARRIVED in Detroit one gloomy afternoon after an exasperating drive through snow, sleet, and wind to find his natal city snowbound and snow silent. Big snow plows were moving through the streets, and traffic was all but at a standstill.

He drove immediately to the Hotel Pontchartrain and was shown to the small suite he had reserved on the fifth floor. William had been in and out of this hotel hundreds of times over the years; in fact, in earlier days it had been a kind of headquarters for many of the young guys he knew. Now it looked a little worn, not quite as elegant as he had remembered.

He wasn't sure just how he felt, beyond a sensation of immense relief to be out of that huge, sprawling, complex, immense, corrupt, and bewildering city on the shores of Lake Michigan. A Chicago writer—Ben Hecht or Carl Sandburg or somebody—had said of Chicago that it was as "dangerous as a city of the European Middle Ages," and that was coming pretty close to the truth. You felt it in the atmosphere; you saw it in the streets, in the eyes of the people; you sensed it at night; and very late at night, in many sections of the town, you didn't like to look over your shoulder. William had suffered from a growing fear over the last few months, and now, in this city of his youth, that fear had entirely disappeared. He felt a strange ease, a strange lightening of the spirit. He had lost the feeling of being perpetually on guard.

But that was only part of it. It was no easy thing merely to walk out on the work and circumstances of a lifetime. William had been in Chicago for nearly twenty-five years; there he'd moved from late youth to middle age; he was Chicago-conditioned. At the moment Detroit merely seemed like a nondescript place of safety, a way station—and yet it was here that he intended now to make a place for himself, as he had made a place for himself in Chicago.

There were relatives he must call, but he was in no hurry about that. One cousin, with a big house at Grosse Pointe, was a tycoon in the auto industry and could probably throw practice William's way, if so inclined. Two other cousins were jointly involved in a large public relations operation with branch offices at Fort Wayne, Indiana, and Indianapolis. He knew little or nothing about this except that both were very prosperous and also had homes in Grosse Pointe.

William was not coming into Detroit like Dick Whittington and his cat into London. He was coming into a cushy spot if he played his cards right and could stand it. William had always considered his relatives a stuffy lot and had fled from them, but the years had passed, he'd grown older—and wiser, he hoped—and it was likely that he had learned a tolerance that had been completely lacking in his early days.

For a while William stood looking down into the snowy streets. Then he shaved, showered, put on fresh clothes, and went down to the formal dining room for dinner.

But this was Detroit, not Chicago, and there was no strong drink available in the dining room. But the maître d' said, rather nervously, that if the gentleman brought his own with him "they could handle that." William did not know what the fellow meant and refused to pursue the point. He felt vaguely depressed. Would he be reduced here to depending on a bootlegger who might sell him anything at all for "choice stuff"? Well, there should be plenty of it about, with the shores of Canada only a stone's throw away.

His dinner was mediocre—it looked like top hotel food but wasn't—and William felt further depressed. He was spoiled, obviously, and all this might take some getting used to. He lit a cigar and sat back with a sigh. No liqueur, and the coffee was at least two removes too weak. The only thing top class about the meal was the price.

William left and strolled about the lobby for want of anything better to do. Snow was falling heavily past the big front windows. He wandered over to the newsstand just as a man in a blue jumper arrived and began to stack some newspapers, out-of-town papers, William noted. He picked out his favorite Chicago paper and went over into a corner where there was a comfortable chair and a good reading light to look through it. He'd just left Chicago, and yet he felt he'd been away for a long time, and the sight of a Chicago paper gave him a pleasant feeling.

Suddenly he sat bolt upright, badly jolted. He'd come to a long story of the "raiding of the West Side brothels," and in the middle of it there was a section on the issuance of new warrants of arrest; and among those for whom warrants had been issued was the name of one William Macready, attorney-at-law.

William turned cold, then hot. At worst he'd expected a subpoena, at best nothing. This just couldn't be. There must be some kind of silly mistake. He looked through some of the other names: Maurice Degnan, Mario Fanelli, then several unknown to him; then Harold Krumpacker, Alois Hruba (the alderman? Good God!), Cyrus D. Travis (who was he?), and then nearly a dozen others unknown to him, women and men, probably madams and their gentlemen employees.

"Well," said William, his sense of humor not completely gone, "I find myself in wonderful company."

And for a moment the shocked face of Daphne rose before his eyes. Daphne was a very correct lady. What would she make of it? Still . . . this was all academic at best.

What should he do? Could he be extradited? An extradition battle was not something to look forward to. So what to do? All thought of a steady career in Detroit was now out the window. Was Canada the next stop? He could just step across, you might say.

And after long thought, William decided that Canada was definitely in the cards.

Good-bye, Chicago!